Citadel 7 Series

Enemy
of
Existence

On Earth

A threat to all Existence looms.
Two Wardens remain, but it's their mysterious apprentice who holds
the key to survival.

Novella 1

Yuan Jur

Cover art : Ralph Manis/Infinitee Designs

Australia

ISBN-978-0-6481977-7-5 (Paperback)

ISBN-978-0-6481977-6-8 (E-Book Epub)

ISBN-978-0-6481977-5-1 (E-Book MOBI)

Cover and art design by Ralph Hawke Manis of Infinitee Designs © 2017

www.infinitee-designs.com

Book design and production by WaaDoom Press in association with

Thebookpatch.com

Editing and structure by Charles Wannop and De Chao Peterson

Dedication

Many thanks to The Citadel 7 Series Crew; Editors John David Kudrick & Mary Rosenblum, compilation and type setting, Charles Wannop—the many proof readers and the beta test group who help the Citadel 7 series reach for the high bar.

Orders

"Welcome Agent. This mission propels us along the Superverse continuum through the endless oceans of Dark Matter. We will emerge in a timeline where some things will seem familiar, others quite strange. The voice of *Central* will now take you through our brief. See you on the ground. Mission success to us all!"

C-DATE: CLASSIFIED.

UNFOLDING TIMELINE: ACTIVE.

MISSION AUTHORIZATION: EVERCYCLE SEVEN.

MISSION POINT OF ORIGIN: SOL STAR SYSTEM, PLANET EARTH.

PLANET SECURITY LEVEL: 10.

LOCAL TIME/PLACE: 1963, AUSTRALIA.

MISSION CATALYST: DETECTION OF RIFT IN LOCAL SPACE TIME KARMA STREAM. WARDENS, UNISS AND DOGG, DISPATCHED TO INVESTIGATE. PERMISSION FOR LOCAL TIMELINE REMOVAL OF MORTAL INDIGENOUS TO THE WORLD–APPROVED.

SOUL CORE CHANEL ESTABLISHED. WARDEN YOU ARE CLEARED TO ADDRESS THE AGENT.

CHAPTER

1

Nothing as it seems

Welcome back, Agent. My name is Uniss. We are on a mission of hope in dark times. We must turn the tide of a cataclysm now threatening us all. Please listen carefully to what I have to say, it is key to our survival and the preservation of all we hold dear. Before we hit the ground, let me ask. Do you remember ever being part of a paradox? I have lived through many. Do we ever meet anyone significant to our lives by chance? Had I known the true threat he posed back then, I would have sent him for erasure on our first encounter. But then, had I done that, none of what has unfolded would have been possible. Hindsight always makes me smile, as do those who use it. Once decorated for valor beyond the call, we have now been thrust forward again and made responsible for setting things right. This mission is not by choice, but then, nothing's as it seems. Bear that in mind, Agent, as the telling of Commander Bloch's tale unfolds, for like you, we are now part of his legacy too.

✳✳✳

Two silver shafts of light struck the sun-scorched red earth and a sound of fine shattering glass arose in a whirl of dust breaking the bushland's silence. The energy dissipated, revealing two gray-clad, war-hardened intercosmos travelers. Standing beside his companion in the heat and dust of the arid land's mid-afternoon sun, the brim of his Warden Profiler's weathered gray hat wavered in an irregular eastbound wind. For their return, he'd kept his preferred form as a half-caste Aboriginal of the local human race. Eyes clearing, he lifted his view and surveyed the windswept topography with a knowledge that went far beyond the mid-forties façade he projected. He considered this mortal world's *true* function and the future purpose of all incarnates in residence on this world. Then he sighed considering what might have to be done.

There's a catch, there's always a catch, he thought.

In his right hand, he held an aging rolled parchment, a decree for all humanity written by Zero, the Lord of Life's Spark, head of the Citadel Superverse Council, and original creator of Superverse existence. The decree validated the two Warden's presence in this world and their authority to make any changes to this world's time line they saw fit. A tiny alarm sounded, and the Warden pushed back his sleeve to expose his Continuum chronograph wrapped around a tanned wrist.

"We're good to go," he said to his scruffy canine companion. He looked skyward. "They're almost here."

Uniss bent and pulled a grass stem from the ground next to his right boot and then pressed the sprig between dry lips while contemplating their mission directive. He heard a rustle in some nearby tussock grass. From the corner of his eye, he glimpsed a large black snake slithering into the grass root shadows.

"Now that's a sign," he said to himself and looked to his companion. "If our replacement turns out to be a doppelganger—and I suspect he is, Dogg—this is the end of the line. If I get taken out before I can locate and deal with his handler, see that he at least is processed for full erasure, immediately."

"Okay," said Dogg.

"And, Dogg. Don't go all Buddha on this one like the last potential replacement. If they don't work out, they have to be erased. This one's our last hope. We'll deal with Lord Zero and the Council later."

"Uniss, I know my part," Dogg said, flicking her left ear to get rid of a large bush fly. "Maybe *this* replacement will shine some light on how to stop the coming reset. I realize, if we don't find an answer through them, there won't be a space time continuum around, period."

He unrolled the parchment, thinking on the first words exposed.

"I hear that," he said.

Uniss's heavy shin-length duster buffeted against lean strong legs as the decree flapped in his grip from a gust of wind threatening to blow it away.

"We best get to it then. I hope this world still has enough integrity to withstand what's coming."

Looking to the horizon, drawing a deep breath for the pronouncement's delivery. He prepared as if his announcement were intended for some vast invisible listening audience. Reverently, Uniss delivered the declaration in his husky baritone way.

"From Lord Zero, to the caretakers of this world: "Remember . . . there was a time when gods walked the Earth with man in league to watch over the prisoner and keep him dissolved. Outside Earth in the black stands Tyr, guarding the gates, keeping all hemmed in.

But as ages have passed and histories were written, and gods one by one became fable and man corrupt, the prisoner, Herrex the Destroyer, first fallen of nine, built armies little by little and walked Earth freely in the dreams of those left behind.

Armies of thoughts, flesh and bone, trees, flowers, and even the air all became absorbed under the hand of Herrex, the Lord of Balance.

This is why you have dreams both good and bad of what you must do to hold power. Sometimes, we whisper from far away, trying to take back what we once fought so hard to contain.

Now, on Earth, all the keys you have lost, as you have found many things that lead you astray, being steered by the wind of your dreams, and we gods become stories told only by words of a few.

Truth has long passed. Man thinks he's in charge as Herrex pulls string from behind, smiling at his blind prey, playing warden for their stay as they are unaware of being fooled and kept blind. So, remember the truth behind that itch that lies in the back of your mind . . .

Who am I really? Where do I come from and why am I here? Why do I remember what has never appeared, and why do I believe in what my eyes have not seen?

Earth Clan! Ask yourselves this! What if rebirth is real? What if belief, birth, death, and all such play are the doorways to other places?

What if every person, animal, and independent life on Earth contributed to the balance of a greater Superverse, a place where man has a most important job?

If for a second you feel this, read on, then look around, for your existence is magnificent."

The words of Warden Uniss ended replaced by a whistling gust of wind. He looked down to his stocky companion.

"Hope the message carries as far as it's supposed to, Dogg. We can do with all the help we can get."

Uniss re-rolled the declaration and placed it back inside his duster's pocket. A sonic boom sounded in the far distance from behind and he looked over his shoulder.

"Can you feel them on comms, Dogg? They're with us now. G'day, Agent! I hope the brief Central gave set you in the right direction. Pleased you finally found the right book cover to open again. It's a strange way in I know, but it's how Superverse integration for anyone from the outside works, and, it's the only safe one. You've been granted access to help us set a serious situation right. Don't worry. Your part in this is about to be made clear. I'm Uniss, by the way. Warden Profiler for Superverse Karmic Admin Adjustments. You remember me, right? We *have* met before. What about my partner here at my feet, Dogg, you remember her, don't you? No? Oh dear."

"They'll have typical, temp memory loss from the Soul Core transfer, Uniss. It'll probably take a week."

"Now, Dogg. Give the Agent a chance. Stepping from their world to our dimension knocks the best of everyone at times. Come on, Agent . . . take a breath, think. You must remember, we travelled across the Space Time Continuum together for a decade or so last time. You even stood at the center of Cobalt's belt."

"Agent, look at me. It's Dogg. I was the last one you spoke to before we sent you back last time. You said you had just the best time, even though we scared you half to death for a lot of it. Surly you remember that? Look at my face. Blue Heeler by breed, Higher Being by nature was the last thing you said before you left. Umm . . . how about when we took you to… Cluster 47? When we were there and you helped stop Starlin from using the continuum sub-gate to enter this dimension, you said I had to be the coolest four-legged canine in existence. Group hug moment, remember?"

"Step closer to them, Dogg. Come on, Agent, think."

"What about the missing tip on my right ear? You always said it made me endearing. My blue-gray fur? Still nothin'?"

"It could take weeks, Dogg. Look at their expression. They won't remember anything until the brain haze from the metta jump clears.

"Ignore Uniss, Agent. He's still testy after that argument at Juno Bridgeport customs last time the three of us crossed back into the M System Continuum timeline.

"Give me a break Dogg. I'll explain as we go along."

"By all means, Uniss. Please explain to our covert Earth Side contact why the clues that *you said* would lead us to those who caused all our problems, instead led us to a whole lot of nothing—again."

"Sarcasm doesn't fit the cute puppy profile you're ploddin' in, Dogg. Those clues were valid then and you know it!"

"Fine, just tell 'em what they need to know for our mission here then, so we can grab who we came for and fix this mess. I want my life and body back. Being sentenced for erasure over some god-complex-holding manipulator's machinations, isn't tickling my fancy in the least."

"Keep your fur on, Dogg. Let's all start movin' toward the pickup point then, okay. It's south of that rise in the mid distance. Arguing now isn't going to help any of it. Sorry Agent."

Uniss avoided a tussock cluster and led the way. "Watch your step and follow me, Agent. Listen up. As of now, you're a key part of what's unfolding in Superverse events. It's okay, we get it. You can't remember much. Happens each time we bring you back. Just watch out for snakes in the tussocks around here while you're puttin' your feet down. It's the season for them here. Come on, Dogg . . . pick your paws up. We've still a fair distance to cover if we're to reach the asset in daylight. Agent, just so you've got your bearings, we're in scrub-lands quite a few hours inland from the east coast of the continent now called Australia. It's the year 1963 on their local time line. Simple place, low tech by Superverse standards. As the crow flies, we're heading northwest to a road a bit of a slog from here."

"My feet still hurt from our last trek, Uniss—and I'm thirsty."

"Well then, you shouldn't have chased those Marmarks on Juno for hours to blow off steam, as you put it, should you? Now stop complainin', Dogg. I need to put the Agent's head right. Sorry, Agent. We should find who we're lookin' for near the base of those hills on our left." Uniss, ignored Dogg's loud sigh. "We're about halfway between a small human township called Tibooburra and a larger place called Broken Hill. Race and attitudes are divided in a variety of turbulent ways for the local peoples. Many hold a point of view blind to what's truly right or wrong regarding the bigger picture for this planet's well-being. It's part of the reason this planet's inhabitants were cut off from the rest of the Superverse from the start. The human worldview is still too narrow for what's swimming around in the greater cosmos. Ya see, Agent, we wanted to tell you this back on Juno, but too many unwanted eyes and ears there. And adhering to Citadel Evercycle Council protocol made it difficult. Dogg and I are under contract to the Citadel Evercycle Council. The Council as we've told you before is responsible for existence. Then the argument happened over how much you *should* be exposed to and we had to send you back in a hurry when Admin got involved."

"He means for everything in existence existing in the first place, the big bang and all that."

"Yeah, thanks, Dogg. On our Citadel rankings we're called 'Warden-profiler.'"

"Until we were suspended anyway."

"Thanks, Dogg. I know we promised we'd be safe back then, Agent, but it didn't work out that way. We still call ourselves 'profilers' since we're on official business. We're sort of middle management. Some realms label us as lesser gods; others call us Cosmic Lords."

"I feel more like a janitor."

"It won't be for long, Dogg." Uniss sighed. "Ever since you've been unable to retrieve your true form, you've gotten grumpier by the minute."

"It's fine for you, you can step out of your meat sack any time you like. It was me saving your neck last time that got me stuck with this body."

"You're right. I'm sorry, Dogg. We'll undo what Zharkaa did to you soon as possible. Now will you shut up and let me finish?"

Dogg looked away and trotted off.

"I feel bad about what happened, Agent, but there is little I can do to help her get her true form back right now. Profilers such as Dogg and me represent part of a super-sentient race called Filion. We can take many forms, occupying different hosts. Warden Profilers work in independent roles usually . . . well, except for Dogg and me. We are, or were the only registered permanent partnership after the end of the Citadel Wars. Our race never needs rest, unless mortally wounded, are always focused, and are absolutely impartial in making karmic decisions concerning the Council's interests, right, Dogg?"

"Piffle."

"Not helpful, Dogg. Our original vocation was to determine who goes to the next rebirth cycle and who stays in a holding pattern awhile longer. All profilers, Agent, follow the protocols of upper management to the letter . . . don't we, Dogg?"

Dogg rolled her eyes.

"It all worked that way originally, until Evercycle Herrex, Lord of Balance, went rogue and was incarcerated for trying to bring about a complete existence reset. See, Agent, in some respects, existence itself is alive. The God's Senate even gave it a name, Morphosis. Existence must breathe, just as all the living incarnates inside it do. Lord Herrex's job was to keep everything in balance. Instead, he took his power and used it for his own selfish ends. So, we had to shut him down. Now, while he is . . . away, Dogg and I have been made responsible for the Continuum systems balance, a balance that for reasons we don't understand is slipping away."

"You mean it's in the toilet, Uniss."

Uniss sighed.

"Thanks for the added color, Dogg. Unfortunately, she's right Agent. After Lord Herrex's departure, Superverse evolution became further unhinged. Even Lord Zero, oldest of the Evercycles said he could do little to stop what Herrex had set in motion. And we . . ."

"Enough history, Uniss!"

"Okay, okay. As you're traveling with us, Agent, don't forget that, as before, you are still anchored in your home dimension, but now have one foot in our reality as well. You're a vital observer only, at this time. Have all the opinions you like. But say nothing to anyone here, except us of course. Don't interfere, even in your dreams—not even if you think you can help. If you do, this reality will dissolve in the space time continuum and we'll have no way back or know what is true or false."

"Our asset's metta signal is strong now, Uniss."

"Doin' my best, Dogg. Agent! Watch those tussocks on our left; there's a Copperhead snake in there. Listen, at the beginning of this existence cycle, Lord Zero and the Citadel Council felt it necessary, for reasons beyond our security clearance, to break one single ever-expanding Superverse into ten separated dimensions. We are presently in Citadel 7's jurisdiction which is billions of your light years large in every direction. It is where all reincarnation and sentient evolution takes place. Citadel 7 is usually overseen by Evercycle Seven, but no one has seen them since we last parted company."

"Something's off about that, Uniss, if you ask me. Evercycle Seven is never… absent."

"I agree Dogg, something fishy there. The heart of Evercycle Seven's jurisdiction encompasses the mortal space time continuum or, M system, M for Mortal. Inside it, all life-supporting planets like your Earth have a mirror world in an alternate place and timeline. Earth's mirror is called, 'Tora,' which is a preindustrial world several galaxies and two dimensions away from here."

"Not looking forward to our return visit there after we pick up who we came for. That place is a powder box ready to explode. Still healing from the last stint."

Uniss brushed some flies away from his face.

"That's right, Dogg, and it set us back a piece too to get back in the Council's good graces. Both planets are governed by Citadel 7 Central where the council is situated. That's who you heard on comms earlier and who authorized this next mission. Earth and Tora share a level ten high-security lockdown status that connects them via a dark matter ethereal mortal umbilical. That connection is largely the reason we are here, and why we need the replacement we've come to collect.

"Under Evercycle Seven's watchful eye, all the highest levels of reincarnation traffic for both Spirit-Sider and the Solid Siders, or mortals as you call them are governed. It includes the god echelons, angelic dimensions, and greater demon realms. At one time, all higher races—incorporeal and mortal—interacted, traded, and exchanged culture and knowledge. Unfortunately, the actions of Lord Herrex to take control of existence incited the Citadel Wars and everything changed. Now nothin's as it seems, Agent—remember that."

"Everyone had to pick new sides fast when that happened."

"That we did, Dogg. As you might remember, all Superverse agents, including wardens like us swear allegiance to a particular Citadel house. Each house is governed by one of the Evercycles such as Seven. Earth and Tora were technically placed under Lord Zero's authority after the War trials. Our allegiance is now to him.

The new apprentice we've come to collect is a concern because they are tied somehow to the God of War, Tyr. Tyr is Space Time Continuum Security Chief for the Citadel Council. Recently, Lord Zero summoned them to freeze all further reincarnate traffic for Earth and Tora. That's a really big deal where Superverse evolution is concerned, Agent. In Earth's case, human beings and their free will are key to the planet's karma stream balance, which is now compromised.

If we can resolve the problem, the Council will allow the reincarnation cycle to be restored. We've been set up for all that to wrong. We were ah… volunteered for this mission."

Padding along a few steps in front, Dogg looked back over her shoulder and then hung her head.

"Come on, Dogg, pick your ears up. We'll set things right. I know it's not good that ninety percent of our asset's full past lives Akashic record has been obscured with security black line. But, the clear part of the brief agent Marvin *did* manage to slip us, indicates our new apprentice carries a dark cataclysmic potential."

"And you think this helps us how?"

"Well, Dogg, we know they've been given an alternate identity. We know they're important enough that someone in Central doesn't want us to know what we've got, till it's too late. Think, why would the Council push such a dangerous asset like that our way."

"To step back and laugh at the mess that follows?"

"Right! But what if we can find out who this stooge we've been served up really is? Maybe, just maybe we can use them to clean things up and put us in the clear."

"Well, I suspect that the moment we train our replacement to an acceptable level, the powers that be will have us shuffled off to the Echaa Realms for complete erasure. It's Herrex. He's doing it somehow, I'm sure of it. He warned as much when we locked him up."

"Maybe, Dogg, but we also now know that someone is manipulating Earth or Tora's true reincarnate evolution data. Herrex can't do that from where he's sittin'."

"Right, so someone else is using Herrex's mischief as a blind for their own aims. Everyone just lives and dies to be reborn in a different time slot on the same world over and over. But, the public record says the opposite."

"Yes, it does. We now know all the long-term past life recall records for Earth and Tora have been falsified, and I think this new apprentice is somehow the key to finding out why."

"So, no one on Earth or Tora has any idea what their lives were before the present rebirth? That means they can't plan for a better evolutionary future when their cycle ends."

"Exactly, Dogg. That's why our friend the Agent must know how we got to here. It might also help them remember something we can use so the mistakes of the past are not repeated in the future."

Uniss wiped beads of sweat from his brow with his sleeve and then looked to the mid distance.

"Damn, this place's hotter than usual, Dogg. My host could do with a cool drink about now."

"Not likely till we get to the asset's campsite. How do you think I feel in a dog form?"

"Keep movin' then. Quicker we get there, the cooler we'll be. So, Agent, you now begin to see things are a bit of a mess for the future of the Superverse I hope. Lord Herrex has already cost the Superverse thousands of worlds and corrupted as many realms on his path of destruction. We can't let any more downward spiral happen."

"We're are hardly in the position to be any sort of grand influence right now, Uniss."

"Don't know about that, Dogg. We can keep a lower profile this way. We can use what we learned from looking after Soja Bridgeport while the new Karma Admin Management System was established too. Soja served as the second-highest echelon of Citadel post-war operations, Agent. You remember that, right? Information we got from there is priceless."

"So, it doesn't leave you wondering about our awkward conversation with Evercycle Six, Lord of Boons Good and Bad? How she was suddenly absent shortly after, sent on some dodgy sabbatical evercycles never take? Even Seven didn't know where she went."

"I saw what was going on too, Dogg. The moment Starlin showed up in his reinstated position as Karmic Accountant telling us to relax until further notice, I knew things had turned right sour."

"No one likes Starlin on the best of days, Uniss."

"Nah, he was just the messenger, Dogg."

A gust of wind blew in from the west causing the two Warden's to brace against it.

"I saw the look on his face, Uniss. He enjoyed every minute of our exile."

"Starlin's a sewer snake, Dogg, we both know that. But he's just a tool for Evercycle Three. His influence stops when she does."

"He's got something of his own up his sleeve, I know it. We all spent too many years together to think otherwise, Uniss. He was too smug. He knows what he did to us and those worlds was so wrong. We were sunk from the moment we left the briefing room."

"Starlin'll get his comeuppance, Dogg. He's barely holding favor with the council now. We'll wait for the right time to deal with him. It's Herrex's mother, Three, who's our big worry. She enjoyed every bit of the mischief stirred from the background while all the attention remained focused on Herrex's trial. Good thing we could ensure that many of the problems the war exposed will never reoccur."

"With Herrex gone, the power vacuum that arose will soon force Three's hand that's for sure."

"Agreed. At least we can use this time to deter reincarnate applicants from seeking out those dealing in the black market for karmic futures. Hopefully, we can save a few civilizations before they make themselves extinct, just like the Inca's of Earth did at the start of all this mess."

"It was all working fine until that bean-counter for management in Starlin's old department noticed the higher volumes of traffic we'd stimulated."

"Bastard! They flagged it to be investigated—"

"And Starlin promptly used our actions to his advantage which landed us in it all over again."

"She's right, Agent. Even though Starlin was put on trial, his report on our activities still had sway with the council. That detailed description of the excess positive karma creation on our account near buried us. Our reincarnate traffic tables showed a massive drop in negative karma flow across the Superverse compared to other Citadel Wardens. You might remember. According to Superverse evolution Design Regulation 1002—Acceptable Karma Volume Returns—fluctuations in the reincarnation ratios must show balanced ratios of positive and negative karma for reincarnates. Ours were all positive."

"Yeah. Which Starlin's then doctored further showing the high levels of positive karmic on-flow were harming space time continuum balance."

"He did, Dogg. The Council, on Three's say-so then temporarily reinstated Starlin to his position as Chief Karma Accountant and empowered him to investigate our actions."

"Yeh! Then Starlin sent the full audit on to Evercycle Five's personal secretary, Adonis, and there's no one more bureaucratic and anal in exercising his powers of office than him."

"Sadly, she's right, Agent. Watch out! Scorpion near your left foot. That would have been nasty. Anyway, that's how we became of interest upstairs in

Citadel Council chambers. Once our names were mentioned in the Gods' Senate it was all downhill from there."

"Yep, no coming back from that."

"There is a still a chance, Dogg.

"But Three saw to it that we were suspended, Uniss. The loose cannon she is she ensured we were sent on hazardous acquisition patrol—and while we were absent, she motioned for a formal inquiry, accusing *us* of being integral in the wrongful arrest of her son, Herrex. What a stich-up that was."

"Dogg's right to be angry, Agent. Three further protested that our application of original thought to reincarnate protocol procedure cast a stain on the reliability of all Wardens' given such responsibility. She cited Rule 1 of the Superverse Creation Principles Manual for Self-aware Life Forms–Life isn't a merry dance! We can't allow Wardens to just *choose* a better life for one reincarnate over another. Reincarnates get what they need, not what they want– she demanded this be enforced. There were many nodding heads of the Council showing support for her words."

"Like I said, stitched-up."

"Then with a clap of thunder, Agent, Evercycle Three flung her favorite amendment to the law in for good measure, just to be sure we were toast. Article 67 of the Citadel Council Protocols Manual now states–All Superverse incarnates must have unobstructed access to choose by free will. Beyond that, Agent, how any self-aware life form evolves is subjective. That they evolve by the choices *they* independently make is paramount."

"That one always gets a laugh from the Demon Lords in the hell realms in Citadel 2."

"Anyway, there we were. Three insisted the punishment fit our crime, then accused us of going rogue. It's the most serious crime a Warden Profiler can be accused of."

"She wanted us just gone, Uniss . . . that's what it was."

"For sure, Dogg. But because we showed that everyone who participated in our new approach removed heaps of negative karma according to manual guidelines, the Council stayed their hand."

"Before our new program started, Uniss, the demon realms had backed up to a breaking point. I saw several requisitions for a whole new demonic plane cross my desk."

"Anyway, Agent. After the Evercycle Council heard all allegations, our founding creators passed judgment on us in a public address—the first of its kind for such a case in Superverse history."

"Hypocrites."

Uniss pressed the brim of his hat up with his thumb.

"About fifty million of the biggest movers and shakers of the intercosmos turned up to listen to the verdict, Agent. There wasn't a vacant cloud bench for galaxies. Then, a big surprise to all, Lord Zero appealed to the council for leniency in our defense, citing our exemplary war service as part of the consideration. Evercycles Three and Five, however, would have none of it and demanded a sentence of 'punishment through personal choice of the criminal.' A majority ruled against our favor and Speaker for the Council, the god Achilles, announced we would choose one of two paths. We could either, accept a mission of reconnaissance and world repair from a Council-directed duty list. This, they informed us, also entailed recruiting, training and personally sponsoring our replacement again from a list of candidates supplied."

"That was a list of one, Uniss."

"Just a moment, Dogg. *Or*, two, we could both choose to be scheduled for full erasure from the space time continuum in the Echaa Realm forthwith, and then have any remaining string particles reshaped into something not quite so … rebellious. Stop rolling your eyes. I know it was a no brainer."

"Three offered that second option with real satisfaction."

"The decision has been tough on both of us. All we've done, really, is buy a little time to find out what and who in the intercosmos is behind all the trouble before they are onto us. All we know about our candidate is that he is an Earth incarnate human male. We could only discover one clue as to his background. The individual listed is registered as a relocated prisoner of high rank, one with a Class 7 complete pre-lives wipe. This fella is part of the New for Old Past Lives Treaty. Many Superverse enemies not sent to the Echaa Realms for erasure after trial, agreed to the sentence of a full memory and skillset wipe."

"Do you think it possible our new apprentice is one of those, Uniss? 'Cause if they are, something isn't right. I can't sense this being's core *at all*. It's like he is a karmic vacuum."

"But, what other alternative was there, Dogg? The Agent here projected a similar karmic pulse when they arrived, probly just a glitch on the thread. Earth's karmic pathways are pretty unstable now, Agent. There are a lot of false readings. I'll get back to Fortress of Bach records first chance I get and see what else I can find. Maybe Mortilan can help. This young fella's past lives' record must carry some heavy information to have such limited access given to us."

"If it wasn't for Nine, Lord of Harmony, we'd have nothing, Uniss. Do you remember any of our interaction with her, Agent? You were there when we last saw her too. She hasn't been available since. We'll need to find her soon, Uniss."

"Don't forget Dogg. Five reminded us that doing anything like digging for information without their express authority would break Evercycle Code Six of the Secrecy Act."

"Yeh, I know, bingo, instant erasure in the Echaa realm.

"Right. So, we'll play our cards close to our chest for now. We need to see what the go is with this new apprentice. Come on, this Earth summer heat is going to cripple this body if I don't get it to some shade soon."

CHAPTER

2

Innocent Apprentice

Uniss sighed and looked around the sunbaked landscape as they stepped on toward their objective.

"Custom planets like Earth always have to have their quirks, I suppose, Agent, especially when incarnate mortal platforms are added to develop original free-will and karmic threads, ay Dogg."

"Having the Jenaoin build a custom order like Earth and Tora for the Evercycle Council always is, Uniss."

"Well, this place has gone through several upgrades recently according to records, but I don't see any of it, do you?

"No. but by the looks of the recent geo-scans we've seen, there has been a lot of abuse by the caretakers of Earth's karmic balance. This continent feels one of the hardest hit too."

"I think H must be finding more ways to wear the locals down."

"Or he's had help, Dogg. The new security protocols should make moving around here more difficult for unsanctioned visits, but I sense it's now quite the opposite."

"Hmm, yes, your right. It does feel different now from the last visit, now you mention it."

"Mortal Worlds and General Administration along with Random Selection fall under Citadel Three's jurisdiction now since the shakeup, don't they?"

"Yeh, it does."

They walked on a few paces in silence and then both stopped and looked at each other.

"Starlin," they said in unison.

They stepped on with more purpose.

"If that piece of neutron slag doesn't have his tentacles in this, my tail doesn't wag. Why wasn't that on record?"

"You know why, Dogg. The faster we get off this rock with the new apprentice back to Tora, the better off we'll be. Tyr's last communiqué reports the sun in this star system is increasingly punching raw energy through a hole in the top of the planet's ozone too. My guess is Starlin and whoever is trying to aid H is trying to have Earth declared unstable for further sentient life evolution. That'd force the council to have Zero decommission Earth and they'd have to authorize a new prison for H."

"Yeh. That sounds about right to me. Once that's in flow, it would be a perfect platform to spring H."

"Which means checkmate, if we don't stay one step ahead, old girl."

"You know I hate *that* name too,"

Uniss smiled and looked skyward.

"Look at the color of that sky, Dogg! The caretakers have forgotten their place here."

"You know, I did manage to see a file before we left Central. According to it, House of Three Admin is making cutbacks of species for both Earth and Tora. The file was signed off by Starlin."

"As confident in his position as Starlin is, jigging with the stability of both Earth's and Tora's Superverse stability is a big step, Dogg. Even Starlin would tread carefully about giving H a way to freedom. It's coming from higher up, I'll bet my soul core on it."

"Neither Earth nor Tora will hold up for much longer if this is anything to go by, Uniss. No intercosmos karmic prison can function like this indefinitely."

Uniss nodded and then rubbed his chin.

"Mmm, we'll have to rethink our strategy with the apprentice then maybe, Dogg. The file said he'd been a recent re-karn of Earth's 60's period. He'll be a youth by this time. Earth males of that age are a pretty robust design, impressionable too; we should be able to use that."

"Agreed," said Dogg.

Uniss made his way around some stunted Melaleuca trees.

"You know, Dogg. The air here tastes of Herrex's life-draining causality filaments. I suspect that's what's being used to infect the humans, probably the races on Tora too. Must be using the humans' own free will against them."

"Or, they don't know their soul core is being slowly sucked dry by something or someone virtually invisible. Nothing's been flagged on Central Admin databases. I checked before we left."

Dogg stopped and sniffed the air.

"It's something not of the locals' own making, Uniss. Damn stuff tastes metallic."

"Starts to make me wonder, Dogg. Zero said Herrex's subtle body could remain here indefinitely if need be, didn't he? That's being made impossible, now the caretakers have been cunningly manipulated into behaviors of cupidity, antipathy, and bewilderment. Seems to me they're serving H's purpose just the way he'd like it. But how can he be running the deception? All his atoms have been dispersed in both the Earth and Toran atmospheres."

"Don't know, Uniss. But the Mk VIII human design *does* have the capacity for some truly extraordinary potential."

"Yeah, you're right. Hey. Slow down. There they are, four of 'em by my eye. See their broken-down transport?"

"Yep. Easy-peasy."

"Right, Dogg, steady as we go. Want 'em to see us comin'."

***

Uniss and Dogg walked toward the broken-down vehicle in plain sight. They could see the stranded family had little shelter from the blazing sun.

"Report read correct by the looks, Dogg. The father, Albert Blochentackle, and wife, Margaret, have fallen on hard times. Makes willingness for new change all the easier."

"Agreed. Family report I saw said two youngsters, said their destiny thread is distinctly in the misfortune cycle. Final report update said, the young male is the target."

"Are you sure, Dogg? That's an update from the report I saw. We have to make sure we grab the right one."

"I have no reason to doubt it."

"Hardest hit in the family have been the kids, especially our acquisition called, Ben. Background reports say, he's been enduring a lot of peer group cruelty lately at his school over racial issues. It's all as a result of narrow attitudes and ignorance by the adults responsible for teaching the students. Sad paranoid business. It's really about causality, Agent: causality and karma. Something each of us can't avoid."

"Uniss is right, Agent."

"The father, Albert, trained as a radio technician under *his* father. I read Albert and wife Margaret's destinies combined via random chance meeting at Albert's father's electrics repair shop. Which resulted in marriage and the birth of their two kids."

"File says the family is close too, dysfunctional, though, but close."

"Report describes Albert as having an aloof and suspicious nature. We'll have to set his mind at ease early, Dogg. God, I hate wearin' these new physical meat suits. So awkward and restrictive to move around in."

"Least you can cast off some layers, Uniss. Try being trapped in a four-legged fur ball all the time. I miss using my two-legged body. I won't take it for granted again when I get it back, I assure you."

"Sorry, Dogg. I know it's harder for you after what happened. I see movement at the camp. Best we both get into character!"

Uniss grabbed the seams of his duster and gave his coat a shake to shift some of the dirt.

"One other thing, Agent. From time to time, you'll hear my voice in your head. I patched you in to our network via your universal translator, so you know what's happening beyond the immediate space. Our channel is locked into your mind thread now. We'll be able to see through your eyes as well, which will help a lot. Wardens use this method from a distance when they can't be there personally to see things in real time."

"We'll be your own personal narrator—like last time, remember?"

"Got it! Good. At least that's working Dogg. Remember, Agent. Anything is possible in the Citadel Superverse—right, lead on Dogg."

CHAPTER

3

Strange Liasons

As they drew near the campsite, the hot afternoon breeze tasted thick and gritty to Uniss. He looked skyward as he stepped forward. Even the bush flies that plagued the area here had sought some haven in the shade away from the heat. The road in the mid distance shimmered as though in vapor and the cobbled together campsite could easily have been a heat wave mirage. Uniss noticed a pair of eagles riding high on the thermals above.

That's true freedom, he thought and pulled back one flap of his duster to let air circulate around his legs as he walked. His action revealed a glint from the gold pommel and grip of a fine God Cutter war blade hidden under his coat. Uniss realized it was exposed and reached inside his coat and drew the weapon's scabbard's docking strap tighter and then pulled a small cowl over the weapon's grip to keep it concealed. They passed the broad trunk of a fallen dead gum tree, and Uniss pulled down on his hat's brim to shade his eyes better.

"This'll put everything right for us, Dogg, you'll see."

She looked back over her shoulder at him. Her ears dropped with a sad expression of, 'not likely'.

Uniss watched Dogg swing her view back to the camp site and without a word padded on. That look of hers, Uniss knew well. It expressed the view of one who had traveled the Superverse long enough to know that in the long run, more often than not, nothing's certain till the moment has passed.

"Dogg, give Agent the last of the sting in the circumstance, I mean–so when it's time, the thread can play out."

Dogg's pace slowed.

"If I must. Okay, Agent. I'll make this very quick. Albert and Margaret, that we are about to meet have been married fifteen years. In their mid-thirties now. Just before Margaret contracted a life-threatening illness in months past, she accepted a new position to teach youngsters in middle school. She is to be the new schoolmistress at a bush country town called Broken Hill. That's where they were headed before… well before they had to stop. On her present life thread, she's got about six months left on this world. Albert knows the truth, but they've hidden it from the kids. Albert, very different personality to his wife. Broods on most matters of concern, and there's always been something about his son that bothered him, only he can't quite put his finger on it. We have to find a way to convince their boy to come with us of his own free will, without pinging a warning in Central's Karmic Thread alerts."

Uniss and Dogg could see the family members clearly now. Their aging VW van sat crippled off to the side of the road with one rear wheel jacked up for clearance underneath. The vehicle's faded two-tone green and white paintwork indicated that care and concern for proper upkeep were well past. Apart from one mature gum tree twenty yards away from the vehicle, nothing else provided any real shade within walking distance. Skyward, the two wedge-tail eagles that Uniss had spotted earlier drifted toward the campsite riding the thermals as if they were a symbol of something about to happen.

***

On the ground around the campsite, almost no breeze existed to relieve the heat as the clock passed 2:00 p.m. The Blochentackle family, by the time their transport had sputtered to a stop hours earlier, had found themselves stranded some distance from any help to have it repaired. Their vehicle now sat next to a dilapidated fence perimeter. A rusty thread of barbwire wavering in the breeze hung from a nail on one decaying fence post opposite the vehicle's driver's window. The remainder of a wire spool left by someone long ago intending repairs coiled hazardously at the foot of the post. Like an untensioned spring it threatened to trip anyone up careless enough to cross its path.

Sitting despondent at the back of his vehicle, Albert looked around at the depressingly hot scene. A large blowfly buzzed past his face just missing his nose and he waved a hand at it hitting his own nose instead.

"God dam flies." He looked to the inviting shade under the gum tree. *That's where a man ought to be sitting in this heat,* he thought.

He watched Margaret and the children working together struggling with the ropes of their faded green canvas tent. He sighed and for the third time in the last hour, dragged himself back into the uncomfortable space at the rear of the vehicle between the ground and the engine. He wriggled into position and looked again for signs of the problem.

"You were running perfectly when we left. Why do you cause this grief now?" he said, as if the car should respond.

A piece of warm oily muck fell from the engine and dropped on to his cheek, making him flinch and curse.

"So that's your answer. Keep it up Fritz and I'll trade you in on a Ford first chance, I promise. Then who will put up with you, hmm?"

In the background, he heard his five-year-old daughter, Sally, call out to her mother.

"Look, Mum! There's a doggy and a bush ranger coming!"

Albert stretched his neck trying to see across the road through a gap of spindly grass obscuring most of the view. In the other direction, he looked back to see his daughter standing next to the door flap of their tent pointing into the distance. Her cotton dress fluttered around her knees with a small breath of hot breeze passing by. Wanting to get finished quickly, he put all his focus back to his task.

Meanwhile, over at the tent, Margaret, hearing her daughter's call strained on a rope to finish tying it off. She bent over a tent peg she'd just driven into the ground and tied the slipknot off against it. Then she stood to see what Sally was on about one hand on her aching back. She dropped the slack end of the rope and shaded her eyes with her free hand. Peering into the distance, she followed her child's pointing finger. Yes, two odd figures were indeed coming their way. Both appeared more of a mirage than real as heat waves rose from the ground all around them. Margaret took Sally's hand and walked over to Albert's protruding legs at the back of the VW.

"Bert! Bert!"

She heard Albert groan and saw him lift one knee in a lazy fashion.

"What is it?"

"Someone's coming!"

"I didn't hear a car."

"No. They're on foot."

"On foot, what do you mean, they're on foot?"

Another frustrated groan preceded her husband's retreat from his work-space.

"It's a doggy and a bush ranger, Daddy!" said Sally, running a few steps from her mom.

Awkwardly, Albert pushed himself to a standing position with a grunt, leaving greasy hand marks on the rear bumper.

"Where are they?" he asked Margaret. "Are you sure it's not her imagination flying freely again?"

"There," Margaret said, pointing. "Coming out of the scrub on foot. They must be roasting plodding over the range on a day like this."

Albert pulled his black-rimmed glasses from a top pocket and slung them on with one hand. He squinted and stared into the direction Margaret indicated.

"Oh, yes I see."

Margaret handed him a rag that hung on the open rear door.

"Here, wipe your hands."

Albert accepted the cloth straining to make out the details of the approaching stranger and his dog.

Standing next to him, Margaret wiped a wisp of blonde fringe to one side that had fallen across her face. She moved away a few steps to retrieve Albert's black-banded fedora hanging from the end of a fallen tree branch lying next to the VW. She handed it to her husband.

"Better look your best for our guests," she said dryly.

Albert rolled his eyes, took the hat and pressed it on his head barely covering some of the sweat on his brow. He stared toward the approaching figures for a few more breaths, thinking.

"They are clearly coming directly toward us," he said. "What could they want?"

"Shade maybe, just like we're after," said Margaret.

"See, Daddy, a real live bush ranger!" Sally said.

Albert gave the girl a glance.

"If he is my dear, then he seems to have lost his horse and saddle."

"Who is it, Mum?" called their son, Ben, walking up from behind.

The boy stopped next to his mother, showing a little sunburn on arms exposed by a short-sleeved cotton shirt. A sand-colored grasshopper leapt from a blade of grass, landing on his gray trouser leg. Ben bent carefully to catch it and made a grab for the insect, but it sprung sharply away into the grass again.

"Drat," he muttered to himself.

He stood, one hand holding the broad brim of his brown Jackaroo's hat now sitting crooked on his head. His mother put her hand under his chin to examine the beginning of the sunburn on his fair skinned face.

"We'll have to do something about that," she said.

With a lull in the wind, they all heard the faint sound of the stranger's steps.

"Stay close you two, hear me?" Albert said to the children, wiping more of the mess off his hands with the cloth.

"Yes, Dad," they replied together.

Albert placed himself between his family and the approaching pair.

"Why don't you two go help your mother and clean up around the tent while I greet our guests," Albert said with a relaxed smile to them before giving a more serious glance to his wife.

Both children ran off to the tent, out of earshot.

"They'll be thirsty out in this all day," Margaret said, stepping up beside her husband.

"Let's just be a little careful, shall vee, dear?" Albert said, his German accent thickening as it always did when he felt concern.

He tossed the rag aside. Looking at Margaret with a frown, he went to place a caring hand on her shoulder, stopping when he remembered the grease stain it would leave.

"Are you alright, dear?" he asked. "Is the pain bad today?"

"No, I'm fine. Let's see to these two," Margaret replied with a thin smile.

She glanced to see if the children were paying attention. Albert knew that look. She was lying. Her discomfort had increased significantly of late as her disease increased its grip. Now much closer, the ground swelter gave both approaching figures a slight aura. A few steps behind his dog, the stranger walked toward them with a confident gait. As detail of his form became clearer, his face remained in shadow under the dusty drover's hat he wore. Though it protected him from the sun, its weathered condition suggested the first sign he was not a man of means. The stocky gray Blue Heeler trotting by his side looked like she hadn't had any grooming in a while. Their appearance deepened Albert's apprehension.

"Let me handle this, dear," said Albert, softly.

A cheap collared white shirt under that dusty long gray riding coat and dark tan moleskin trousers covering his legs confirmed he wasn't well off. But, his broad black leather belt with its large ornate shiny buckle wrapped around his waist said something else about him. It looked like one some of the champion rodeo riders they'd seen wore. It caught Albert's interest for a moment. Covering his feet, the stranger wore a pair of sorry-looking stockman's boots that hadn't seen a brush in years.

Maybe little Sally was right, Albert thought. *In another time, the stranger's appearance could have been bush ranger, minus the horse. Could he be carrying weapons under that coat? Oh, dear.*

Albert made a fuss around the vehicle for the moment, keeping one eye on the approaching stranger and his animal, and another on his family. The wind dropped to nothing and the stranger's coming steps seemed to amplify. Closer still, the man appeared to be in his mid-forties, of mixed race with a coffee colored tan. His hair, jet black and curly tight, sat short on the neck, and the stubble on his chin and jaw showed it had been sometime between shaves.

Should I really have them approach at all? "But how can I stop them? Not exactly anywhere to go," he mumbled to himself. "Now it's too late anyway."

***

From the other side of the road, Uniss gave a greeting wave and for a moment raised his head a touch to present a bright-white toothy smile. Then he and Dogg crossed the road casually ready for introductions with the two apprehensive people standing at the back of the vehicle.

When the drifter lifted his head again to show his full face he stood nearly in arms reach. Albert saw that he had a dimple on his right cheek that merged with other subtler lines to give his dark tanned face a kind expression.

Black fella, Albert thought.

The stranger's dog stopped and sat beside his right boot panting, looking straight at Albert.

"Afternoon," Uniss said evenly in his polite educated Australian country accent.

An awkward silence hung for a long breath. Albert failed to respond until the need to cover his apprehension forced him to step forward. He cleared his throat and with a veneer of mustered confidence asked; "Can I help you?"

"My dog's thirsty," Uniss said, looking down at her. "I'd be grateful for a little water, if you could spare some."

Albert opened his mouth to answer, but stalled when Margaret touched him on the shoulder.

"Where have you come from? she asked. "There's not much out here."

Uniss cast a look skyward and then across to the tree in the distance.

"Been a hell of a trek, missus. My horse got spooked by a brown snake on sunrise. Threw me and I nearly got bit myself as my horse bolted off. Silly bugger didn't stop for dust on the horizon. Accident nearly did me and the dog both in. We've walked enough to cross from earth to the moon in last while, I reckon." Uniss looked at the broken vehicle. "Looks like you've got your own problems."

"It's nothing major," said Albert.

"That's quite an ordeal, were you hurt Mr. ah …?" asked Margaret.

Just then Uniss noticed their teenage son wander up in curiosity with his sister following to stand beside their mother. Uniss paid the young man a cursory glance and then focused on the woman again.

"No, thanks missus, nothing my pride can't get past. It's been a while since we sat in the shade, though. Seein' as that gum tree over there is the last decent shade for quite a way, I wondered if it wouldn't be an imposition for my companion and I to sit under it for a spell? Be good to shake the dust out of my boots before we move on."

Uniss waited for a response, being careful not to show too much attention toward the lad next his mother.

Dogg swung a look up to Uniss.

"Uniss, I sense nothing from the girl," said Dogg mind to mind. *"And I'm getting a whole lot of weird from what I scan of the young male."*

"Me too."

"What have they thrown us this time? What help or trouble is he going to be? Looks as if a good breeze could knock him over let alone the trials of a Citadel Warden."

She finished with an audible whine.

Uniss nudged her shoulder gently with his shin.

"That's enough girl," he said in a caring tone. "We're getting it sorted."

"Is the dog friendly?" Margaret asked.

Dogg stood, wagging her tail seeming to understand Margaret's reference to her.

"She's real friendly to any with a good heart, missus. She's good with kids too."

Looking straight at the boy, he knelt to pat Dogg on the shoulder. Ben shaded his eyes with the palm of his hand and met Uniss's stare squarely.

Now there's eyes way beyond the life of the meat and bones he's standin' in, thought Uniss.

The boy tilted his head back and shot his mother a glance before focusing back upon the stranger.

"She's a nice doggy," Sally said butting in and then went to step forward for a closer look.

"Sally!" Albert warned, stopping the child in her tracks.

Unfazed, Uniss stroked Dogg, smiling back at them. Albert noticed the tattoo on Uniss' exposed wrist when his shirtsleeve rode up as he reached to pet the dog's head. Its odd design and coloring reminded Albert of tattoos on some of the old sailors' he'd seen in his youth. But, it was the unusual and expensive-looking wristwatch he wore, that really drew his attention.

The stranger stopped patting the dog's head and pushed his hat up off his brow, exposing his face fully.

"Name's Uniss. This here is my best friend and traveling companion, Dogg."

Little puffs of dust rose from Dogg's coat as Uniss ruffled his hand over her fur. She stood, barked, and wagged her tail happily right on cue. Uniss noticed Albert relax a little.

"I think this heat is taking something out of all of us today," Albert said. "Welcome. My name is Albert, Albert Blochentackle."

Albert took half a step forward and extended his hand. Uniss stood and accepted the greeting in an easy manner. At the contact of the firm handshake, Albert felt washed over with a sudden state of relief, something a tense fellow like him rarely experienced. In a blink, any sense of threat vanished and he felt, well, happy, like he'd just met an old friend.

"This is my wife, Margaret," he said, looking up at Uniss, who stood half a head taller.

The men released the handshake and then Margaret offered her hand and Uniss shook it politely too.

"Pleased to meet you, Mr. Uniss. These are our children, Sally and Ben."

Uniss looked at the two kids.

"G'day," he said.

"What's your dog's name?" Ben asked politely.

Now able to engage with their target for the first time, Uniss and Dogg assessed him closely.

A good-looking but ordinary, fair-skinned human boy. You'd walk straight past him on any ordinary day, Uniss thought. *His façade hides the reality like I've never seen on any relocation asset. Crikey, they've hidden this one well. What dark things were you in your last cycle then?*

"Her name's just Dogg, Dogg with two Gs," he said. "If you were to write it down I mean. She won't answer to anythin' else."

"Does Dogg with two G's like to play?" Sally asked with excitement, swinging the hem of her mother's dress.

"Only if you call her by her name, little miss. She's real smart. Loves games."

Dogg looked up at Uniss. *Look who's calling the kettle black.*

"Come on, Dogg with two Gs!" Sally said, turning to run off.

Dogg stood to follow. After only a couple of steps, Sally stopped and spun on her heels to look at Uniss and then her mother.

"Mum, shouldn't Dogg and Mr. Uniss have a drink first?"

"Yes, Sal, they should, that's a good idea," Margaret said, then looked to Uniss for his approval to let the dog go, which he gave with a nod. "Ben. Take your sister and use the green dish by the tent and the water from the bottle under the seat of the bus."

"Yes, Mum!" the boy said, stepping to take his sister by the hand. "Come on Sal."

Off the two went, with Dogg trotting close beside them.

Uniss looked over at the early model VW Kombi. It looked a tired piece of transport, covered in red dust, encrusted road grim and smudged windows.

Albert stiffened noticeably suddenly aware of the eye of consideration Uniss was placing on the bus.

"It's just a little problem with the thermostat. It's happened before," he said.

"The Thermostat, really," said Uniss. Uniss then raised a questioning eyebrow still looking at the bus. *Not a very good liar,* he thought. *Least he could have picked a mechanical part that actually existed on the vehicle's air-cooled engine.*

It was the distributor cap I fiddled with earlier, said Dogg over the mind link as she followed the children.

"I discovered the fault just before you arrived," said Albert, wanting to appear in control for his family's sake.

The look on his face said he knew the bus was going nowhere though.

"Really?" Uniss said. "Perhaps I can help. I know a bit about cars, specially these German makes. An old German fella I knew was a restorer. Taught me a thing or two about 'em. Terrible for electric faults these things."

"Ah, thank you, Mr. Uniss," Albert said. "But it's too hot now. And I can take care of it soon." He looked to Margaret and saw she looked exhausted. "Come, let's all of us take a spell out of this heat, hmm?"

Albert placed a hand on Margaret's shoulder and turned away from the vehicle stepping off in the direction of the tree offering welcome shade. He gestured for Uniss to take advantage of it with them. Uniss accepted the invitation with a smile and followed on.

"A German engineer, you said?" asked Albert looking over his shoulder.

"He was a ship's carpenter actually. Restoring things like that bus of yours back to showroom condition was his passion. He called himself a 'cargician', mostly when he was drunk."

Margaret had a small chuckle at the comment.

"That's very interesting," said Albert. "German engineering is the finest in the world, you know."

"Really," said Uniss, looking back over at the road-worn bus. "It's been a big day for all of us then."

"It will be fine," Albert said, gesturing to the tree. "As I said. I will tend to it later. Please rest. Get zee dust out of your boots, yes?"

***

The two men approached the base of the Scribbly Gum. The shade felt welcome and dappled light through the upper branches cast shadowed patterns upon the leaf-covered ground. Margaret walked up with two hemp bags from a box by the tent.

"It's not a lounge chair," she said with a smile. "But it'll keep your seat from being numb."

She handed a bag to Uniss and then one to Albert. Thanking her, both men chose comfortable spots near the tree trunk, first making sure there were no Bull Ants nests close by. Margaret excused herself and went off to tend to the children. Uniss sat with his back against the tree, one leg bent at the knee and the other leg extended straight. It was only then he visibly relaxed. Albert spread his bag upon the ground too a couple of steps away and reclined. Uniss removed his hat and set it on his bent knee. He then slid his first boot off with a bit of a groan and a sigh. A trickle of reddish sand, and fine gravel fell to the ground from inside his boot when he upended it. His exposed foot displayed a well-worn sock with a generous hole in the big toe.

"Do you have far to go from here?" Albert asked, casually looking at the ground wiping his brow with a cotton hanky taken from his pocket.

"A fair way, as the Crow flies," Uniss said, pulling off the other boot and dropping it with a clunk to the ground.

"You said the one who taught you about VWs was a ship's carpenter," said Albert. "My father was in the navy."

"Really! You don't say," said Uniss. "When was that?"

"Yes, he was the radio man on a ship called, Cormorant."

Uniss straightened against the trunk of the tree. The comment interested him. His brow crimped in a broad frown.

"Cormorant, a German raider, right?"

Albert's face lit up with surprise. "Ah, yes. You've heard of it?"

"Sure did. A friend of mine was on the Australian war ship HMS Sydney when the Jerry Cormorant sunk her. Lost all hands, I seem to remember."

Albert's shoulders dropped.

"Yes. A sad business. I'm sorry for your loss. I didn't realize the Blacks were allowed to serve in the War."

"Not all my friends are black, Albert," Uniss said looking straight at Albert.

Albert shuffled a little, clearly uncomfortable by Uniss's rebuff.

"But, there are those who were and served as well, and made a bloody good account of themselves too."

Both men looked at each other, sizing up the situation.

"Sorry. I wasn't aware," said Albert. "As a youth, I spent most of the war in the Victorian war prison facility of Grey Town. They rounded up all the Germans, Finns, and Japanese when war broke out, and sent us there. It left its mark you might say."

Uniss nodded.

"No worries, mate. I get it. We should all be measured by the sum of our hearts, not the color of our skin or mark of our country's predecessors I reckon. Too many lost more than their shirt in that one."

"Yes, yes. We did," said Albert, relaxing again.

"Would you like some water, Mr. Uniss?" Margaret asked as she walked up again carrying two tin cups in one hand and a large stone jug of water under the other arm.

"That looks heavy, missus," Uniss said reaching out. "Let me help."

"Thanks," she said letting Uniss take the jug. "Keeps the drinking water colder longer out here."

With a bit of   a look of   fatigue and a puff, Margaret handed them each a cup and then left them to their conversation.

"Where were you headed before your unscheduled stop?" Uniss asked.

"To the only next town possible from here: Broken Hill of course. Why?"

"When I passed the vehicle, the smell of that burned engine oil. That usually means there's not a lot of life left in the engine."

"German engineering is the finest in the world. Fritz has many good miles in him yet."

Uniss looked over at the crippled car with the large VW badge stamped into its nose and then back at Albert with a vague expression of doubt on his face.

"Yeh, you mentioned that."

Albert shrugged a little looking uncomfortable.

"Well, I admit it needs a good service. I'll make it like a new penny again as soon as we are settled in."

"Hope your ah … Fritz sees that day," Uniss said, trying not to smile. "So, you're movin' house then?"

The conversation broke when, in the distance, they heard Dogg yapping playfully with the kids who giggled with all the fun. Twiddling a stick between his fingers, Albert looked across his shoulder watching them with caring eyes.

"Yes, a job opportunity was offered to my wife and things were slow where we were, so off we went."

"What's your missus do then?" Uniss asked.

"I'm a school teacher," Margaret said, hearing his question walking into view from the blind side of the large tree trunk.

Fanning her face slowly with a folded newspaper, she walked over to sit down beside her husband.

"Where does *your* family live, Mr. Uniss?" asked Margaret.

"Originally, a galaxy away from here, missus. Nah, the only real family to me now is, well, Dogg, I reckon."

A cooler breeze rustled the leaves on the ground around them, above some Currawongs sounded off in the swaying upper branches. Margaret looked skyward.

"Thank goodness it's cooling down," she said, still fanning herself.

As Albert looked to the birds flitting about in the branches above, Uniss examined Margaret's face carefully for a moment.

Inspiring to see anyone in such pain enduring it with such grace, he thought. *Made all the worse when she has so much to give and so little time if help doesn't come soon.*

The pleasant moment broke when Dogg charged in from the right with the kids close behind and leapt at Uniss soaking wet and covered in brown dam clay. She landed with a thud in his lap and almost bowled him over wriggling like a fish out of water. Threshing about in a whirl of legs, head, and tail, Uniss could barely contain her. Water and red muck flew in all directions, mostly over Uniss. Her prank included Uniss's face receiving a sloppy enthusiastic licking. He barely managed to snatch his hat out of her way. Jerking back to avoid her playful assault, Uniss hit his head on the tree trunk. Dogg's antics shifted everyone's emotion to laughter.

"Aw, Dogg!" Uniss said.

Both kids laughed themselves silly, which proved infectious for the adults too.

"She found a dam!" Ben said, laughing, mud on his shoes and legs. "It's still pretty full. Sent a brown snake runnin' for the hills too."

"She's very clever, mom," Sally said, giggling and skipping about nearby. "She can play hide and seek wiff the stick, I lost three of them!"

"Not clever enough to have herself a bath alone, I reckon," Uniss said, trying to push Dogg off. "Ah, ya flea hotel, go on, off you get!"

Uniss gave her a shove and Dogg landed, feet tight together, then she spun about before crouching chest low, tail high and wagging.

"Fleas, ooo yuck," Sally said, screwing up her face and rubbing her arms. "They make ya itchy."

Dogg barked and shook her head in play, seeming to enjoy the lark most of all. Uniss brushed at his coat and trousers, attempting to get rid of the mess.

"Well, it will be dark soon," Albert said, after a chuckle. "Ben, you and Sally come help me to get some wood for the night fire. Let's leave Mr. Uniss to that rest he said he needed."

"Okay, Dad," said Ben.

Albert gave Uniss a nod, stood and went off a short distance to gather some wood with the children. Uniss bid Margaret good afternoon and pulled his hat brim down to sleep for a while.

"I think Albert was right. I need this rest more than I thought."

***

Later that afternoon;

Uniss was awoken by a shuffling sound close by. He opened his eyes a crack to see Margaret relaxing. Propped up by her elbows she lay on an old picnic rug enjoying the cooler gentle breeze now blowing in from the east. He watched her arch her neck to look at the sky through the branches above.

She's truly beautiful, in her own way, he thought and took a careful look around for the others.

There, in the short distance, Albert and the two children fussed around a rabbit warren with Dogg playing her part well as always. Uniss sat up and placed his hat on his head. Pushing the brim up an inch he focused on Margret.

"If you don't mind me sayin' so, missus, you look pretty… uncomfortable. Are you alright? When did you start feelin' ill?"

Margaret tried to look as though his comment had little impact and kept her view away to the distance.

"Sorry to disturb you, Mr. Uniss. I didn't know you were awake. It's just something I have to deal with now. It'll pass."

Her cheeks suddenly looked a little flushed. Uniss straightened from his slumped position and stretched.

"That doesn't sound like an easy load, by your tone I mean. Sometimes, some burdens are best shared to find a way out I've found. If you don't mind me askin', how long have you been ill then?"

Clearly affected by his pressing question, Margaret turned her face toward him trying to remain deadpan. In that small moment when their eyes met, her brave façade broke and her expression reflected an unwanted secret discovered. She waited for a long moment and then rolled onto her side and shook her head faintly.

"It's funny," she said.

"What's funny, missus?" Uniss asked.

"You're right. We only just met. You coming out of the bush a small while back like that helped in some way. Now I feel I've known you for years. How can something like that happen?" she asked herself and then sucked her bottom lip a little nervous. "Why *does* wanting to unburden the worst in one's life to a total stranger seem so much easier at times than to those closest?"

"Something's got hold of you missus, hasn't it?" asked Uniss.

Margaret sighed and nodded.

"Six months at best, they reckon is all I have. Apart from Albert, my doctor, and now you, no one else knows. The kids have started asking questions, though. Seeing me tired all the time I guess."

"Real sorry to hear that missus. No way to fix it, then?"

She shook her head slowly.

"Nope. I've even said prayers. Haven't done that for years. Don't think anyone heard me, though."

"Aw, I reckon you were heard loud and clear. Universe is a strange place, missus—my old dad always said—it's got ears and feelings everywhere."

She looked to see where the others were, worried they might hear.

"Is it that obvious now? I worry the kids will see too much," she said, eyes down in a softer voice.

"Nah, missus. You cover it well. Need a real good eye to see through you. I've seen a lot in my time is all. Got to where I could see into people more than they'd like after a while I guess. Some folks say I'm annoying like that."

Uniss straightened his back stretched his arms. Margaret's eyes began to well up with tears and she pulled a hanky out of her dress pocket pretending something bothered her nose.

"Don't worry, missus. Ya never know just how the sun might shine tomorrow, even though things look stormy at dusk the day before. Hey, I hear that dog of mine comin' back."

Margaret looked past Uniss beyond the tree trunk to see the others returning. With an armful of more wood, Albert and Ben walked over to a circle of stones pushed into place earlier to form the makeshift fireplace. Ben dumped his armload on the pile they had been building ready for cooking the evening meal. Sally, dragging a single long thin stick behind her walked up and threw it on top of Ben's pile. She looked at the others dusting off her hands looking satisfied at a job well done.

"Well," Margaret said, standing and brushing some leafy refuse off her dress. "Guess I'll get some things ready for dinner, then. You're welcome to join us, Mr. Uniss."

"Ah, thank you, missus. Just the company, and maybe a cup of black tea 'round the fire will be fine, if that's okay?"

She nodded.

"Well, you're welcome. I best get started. Come on, Sal, you can help."

"I have some things to tidy up around the car too," Albert said. He looked to his son. "Give me a hand, Ben?"

"Okay!" the boy said and followed his father toward the bus.

✷

For the next while everyone shuffled about seeing to various jobs. Uniss collected more wood for the fire, while Dogg, who felt exhausted after her afternoon's entertainment with the children, lay beside the fireplace on her back, legs up, snoring.

Come 8:30 p.m., it had cooled down. A gentle fire flickered with a pot pushed into the hot ashes on the side. With the meal ended, a few stories were exchanged, much to young Ben's delight. Albert told Uniss a positive version about their need to move from Saint George, unaware of Margaret and Uniss's earlier exchange. With some pride, he remarked again about the great new job Margaret had been offered as schoolmistress for Broken Hill primary school. He explained how he looked forward to starting a little radio shop there of his own and most importantly, how he'd be teaching their son a trade in radio and appliance repair, just as *his* father had.

"Ben will be a fine technician in the family business. Isn't that right, my boy?" Albert asked his son with a large smile.

"Guess so," replied Ben, his view skyward with a fixed interest on the stars.

Uniss heard no enthusiasm in his reply as Ben sat on a large fallen branch on the other side of the fireplace.

On this night, a half-moon stood high in the sky. Thin wisps of cloud stretched like worn silk partially obscuring the ocean of stars behind. Somewhere unseen, in the distance a lone Mopoke made its night call.

"There are so many stars!" Ben said. "I'd give anything to go there someday."

The lad's father shook his head, but didn't look up from prodding the fire with a stick.

"You keep your mind in the real world, young man, instead of those stories you keep scratching on paper. No future in that."

Ben ignored his father.

"Gazing up in the sky daydreaming about going to impossible places will get you nowhere either. Don't you agree, Mr. Uniss?"

Ben flicked a quick glance across to his father, looking wistful, and then on to Uniss, who appeared not to be paying attention. Then Ben noticed something glitter on Uniss's shirt.

"Hey, Mr. Uniss," Sally said speaking up through a yawn, head on Margaret's lap noticing the same thing. "Those shiny things pinned to your shirt collar look like stars."

"Do you know much about the stars, Mr. Uniss?" Ben asked ignoring his sister's interruption.

Dogg, lying near Ben, raised an ear and opened one eye to focus on the exchange. Sitting on a stump twiddling a bit of long grass, Uniss pushed the tip of his hat up and looked at Ben.

"Well, where I come from, young fella, stars have many meanings. You could travel this entire life the world over and not see 'em all. Least not from the ground anyway. Some of 'em are only reflections of somethin' from long ago and not even there anymore. Others, well they'er just startin' out and we can't see 'em here yet. For most ov'em, numbers aren't enough to convey the real distance they are away from this world."

"Where did you learn your astronomy?" Albert asked.

"Well, when I was a young fella, my father sent me to stay at a place where a kind of professor of astronomy lived for a while. He took a shine to me and made me his apprentice you might say. Showed me a lot of things. He had a sort of big observatory where we could look through his telescopes to places most eyes would never know about down here." Uniss pointed to the heavens. "He loved to use those telescopes and look at star maps and the like often as possible. Showed me the ways of the heavens as he understood them."

"I've seen stuff flying up there sometimes," Ben said. "They look like long streaks. Like someone took a paintbrush to the sky."

"Well, you're in the right part of this world for it, young fella. Some of the best night sky to look at the stars is right here. There's lots of things floatin' around up there you never expect. Some say, maybe even space craft from other worlds."

"Oh, now that's a bit of a stretch, Mr. Uniss," said Albert. "Stop teasing the boy. The lad has enough silly things filling his head, don't encourage him."

"Oh, I don't know, Albert," said Uniss. "My ancestors have walked this land for more centuries than the white fella who claimed it as his own has a mind to comprehend. History passed down says there are races so advanced by human standards up there that they'd be inconceivable to the average man on Earth, even now."

Albert chuckled. "Sounds like there are dreamers in your family, too, Mr. Uniss."

Dogg saw Uniss's expression shift hinting a more serious mind set for a moment, but it then changed back quick as it had appeared.

"Well, you know, Albert," Uniss said, leaning forward. "I think you're right in the first part. Both my father and my elders, too, I guess, are all dreamers. It's part of the reason we've survived so long here. My dad always used to say; *'those who dare to dream can change the course of destiny.'*"

Uniss waited for Albert's reaction, watching Ben from the corner of his eye. A short awkward silence prevailed.

"All that said, Albert, I came to a conclusion," said Uniss.

"Yes. And what was that?" Albert asked, skepticism obvious in his tone.

"Even without irrefutable proof, it's arrogant and juvenile to believe we are the only creatures of substantial intelligence in the galaxy we call the Milky Way. Something so vast that it would take any man many many life times to cross, must have equal and greater examples of sentient life too that we experience here." Uniss looked at Ben. "We are sitting on a mostly water covered rock that just happens to sit in the sweet spot of an orbit around a sun illuminating a tiny solar system. The cosmos is far too big for there *not* to be other life out there, Ben."

Dogg raised her head wondering how far Uniss would push the subject.

"The arrogance of thinking otherwise will see man on Earth left behind when he should have a front row seat traveling the stars, one day. I'd be more concerned about what beings from the stars might have to say about us. If they have the technology to cross the stars, you can bet they have the ability to listen in on much of what we think and say." Uniss pointed skyward again. "Even if we can't see them, young fella, doesn't mean they ain't there."

"Yes," said Ben in a hushed tone, clenching a fist as if he'd won something good.

Uniss watched Albert's face harden at hearing an adult state such an absurdity as if it were incontrovertible fact. He also noticed how Ben's eyes widened with intrigue and anticipation to know more.

"I think," Albert said, "that you have been walking for too many miles out here in the hot sun, Mr. Uniss. And you shouldn't put such notions in a young man's head. One should work with practicality, what can be seen, not some musings of little green men in flying saucers from Mars."

"They are not green and don't use saucers," Uniss said, poker-faced.

Uniss noticed the smirk and intent to laugh on Margaret's face she tried so hard to conceal, watching her husband's rigidity being played like a fish on a line. Uniss smiled and waved a hand as a gesture of letting the joke pass. Albert's stiffening posture relaxed and he pushed a laugh forward, letting the matter rest.

Just then Uniss suddenly looked as though he remembered something. He reached inside the pocket of his coat and pulled out two collar pins just like the ones he had on. Each measured about the size of a man's little fingernail. Gold flecks mixed in with what appeared to be an opal stone that sparkled in the evening light. Everyone became very curious at what he had in his hand.

"I tell ya what, young fella!" Uniss said with a smile. "You and your sister seem like real good kids. If your dad 'nd mum don't mind, I'd like the both of you to have one of these. They were given to me by my father, when I was young'. I have no family to speak of now, we'll, except Dogg of course. So, I think it's the right thing to do. They'll bring ya both luck, I guarantee."

Uniss held out the pins for all to see.

"Oh, Mr. Uniss," Margaret said, "you shouldn't. That's too generous."

"I'd like to, missus, really. It's always good to give when you can, I always think, and like I said, they'll bring the kids good luck. Every bit helps, right."

Margaret looked to her husband to supply some remark of thanks.

"Ah . . . that is most unexpected. Thank you, Mr. Uniss," said Albert.

"You're welcome, Albert. It's my and Dogg's way of saying thanks to you and your missus for sharin' the campsite and making us feel welcome. So here you go, young fella."

Uniss held the pins out in his palm toward Ben, who stood, and stepped forward to accept the gift. Ben looked at his father, who gave the boy a nod.

"Be sure to give the other one to your sister," said Uniss.

Ben nodded and took both pins giving one to Sally.

"Mind your manners, lad," Albert said.

Ben rolled his pin between thumb and pointer finger watching it glint unusually bright against the firelight for a small moment. He looked back to the sky and raised the pin up high.

"It shines just like the stars! Thanks, Mr. Uniss."

Ben went and sat back on the log near the fire, examining the pin closely.

"What a wonderful night this has turned out to be with such unexpected company," Margaret said through a yawn. "It's getting late, time for bed I think. Kids come on."

"I'll turn in too, I think," Albert said. "Got an early start in the morning and a car to repair."

"Yeah, us too," Uniss said, looking around for a spot to lie down. "I'm sure I can help with that car problem when we are up and about, Albert."

Albert said nothing at first, but then gave a small nod of agreement. "Thank you."

Margaret stood, cradling Sally in obvious distress. Seeing that, Albert stood as well.

"Let me help, dear," he said, and took Sally from her arms and then made his way to the tent.

"You look pretty strung out, missus," Uniss said. "Rest well. A good night for dreamin' of a brighter future."

"Thanks again for your kindness, Mr. Uniss. It's been a long day, but I'm grateful for how it has turned out."

"Things will be fine in the mornin', missus, you'll see."

She turned and headed for the tent. On her way, she slowed and glanced back over her shoulder.

"Good night, Mr. Uniss. Come on Ben. Bed time," she said.

Ben stood and walked past Uniss to follow his mother.

"Night, Mr. Uniss," he said.

"Night, young fella," Uniss said with a grin. "Hope them dreams to walk amongst the stars one day come true."

Ben smiled walking on. "Me too."

Soon Albert returned to the campfire with a bedroll.

He dropped it where he had a mind to sleep and sat back down slowly. He looked at Uniss for a moment as though he wanted to get something off his chest, but then aborted.

"Time for me to shut my eyes too, I think."

Albert unrolled the bedding and stretched out on it near the fire and then rolled over with his back to Uniss. An ember cracked with a pop-bang in the fire.

"Wouldn't sleep there, Albert," Uniss said a hint of warning in his tone.

Albert rolled back over sharply.

"Why not?" he asked, sitting half up and looking at Uniss suspiciously.

Uniss pointed to the overhanging branches above. Albert looked up and a small slender twig fell and bounced harmlessly off his forehead to the ground.

"See that big half-dead branch up there?" Uniss asked pointing.

Albert squinted to see through the branches at the barely visible threat twenty feet above him overhanging the campfire.

"Yes, what of it?"

"These Gums have a habit of dropping branches in the early morning when they are old in this area. And this tree is very old. Could ruin the rest of ya days, know what I mean?"

Albert stalled in thought for a moment, watching the branch. Then, without a word, he got up and dragged his bedroll out of the way. Laying down again, he turned away from Uniss and the firelight. It didn't take long before the campfire had dwindled to embers and all about fell dead quiet. By the time an hour or more had passed, only the soft sleeping noises of resting people could be heard, all except Uniss and Dogg, who never really slept.

At 11:00 p.m. sharp, the faint breeze that had been so comforting ceased and the calling night birds stopped too as if something was about to happen. On the edge of the camp firelight, Dogg opened her eyes and sat up. Uniss lifted his hat and quietly did the same. They looked at each other and then to the sleeping Albert. Uniss nodded to Dogg and she silently slipped away into the shadows.

Albert stirred for a moment as Uniss stood and then went further into a deep sleep, giving an occasional snort and murmur from some dream.

Big day tomorrow for everyone, Uniss thought, looking up at the stars.

Dogg returned a minute later and stood close by the sleeping man. For a moment, she focused on Albert and then gave him a sniff. Then she looked up at Uniss and they both went to work.

CHAPTER

4

The Interview

The air in the tent smelt thick and stuffy after the heat of the day. Ben and his sister rested easily on either side of their mother, who'd fallen asleep almost as soon as her head hit the pillow. He dozed off for a bit and then found himself wide awake again, his mind a swirl of wonder over the comments Mr. Uniss had made about worlds beyond their own. Hands clasped behind his head, Ben lay there for some time before he fought the descent into slumber again. He wanted to hear more from Mr. Uniss when he was speaking about the heavens by the campfire. Ben thought about how the arrival of Mr. Uniss and Dogg felt like the beginning of something special, an appealing scenario compared to recent times for him and his family.

Many Australians still had little tolerance for those whose family had fought on the other side in the last big war. Only last week, a fellow hurled verbal abuse at Albert from a passing car as Ben and his father walked up the street. *"Jerry bastard, you should all be packed back off to Germany!"* they'd bellowed.

We're as Aussie as any of 'em, Ben thought. *Who the hell is Fritz and Jerry anyway? They must have a lot of relatives abroad with his name bein' yelled out so much. Dad was right, that bloke was a blockhead.*

At school, some of the kids had been downright mean to Ben and his sister, just because their father was German. They'd played many pranks and often repeating their parents' racist rhetoric, calling Ben and Sally mongrel German brats. He sighed and rolled his head to look at his mum. He knew she was sick with something bad.

She'd been to the doctors a lot lately. Every time she returned from visiting Doctor Malcolm Reynolds, who was also their only true friend in town, Ben noticed there was some kind of strain between his dad and her. They augured in whispers over mail just opened and he'd seen his mum cry more than once.

He'd asked her about it the day before they left, when she looked so unhappy. But neither she nor his father would say anything, always redirecting conversation to some other subject. She would only say it was not for boys his age to worry about.

I'm grown up, she told me that before, Ben thought, looking up at the dark gently billowing canvas roof.

He listened again outside for any sign of the men still talking and heard nothing but the sounds of crickets and a distant night bird.

Drat.

His mum stirred. Ben shook his head, fighting another increasing tide of sleep. He yawned, remembering the day his mum came home with those two letters. One came from her employer at the education department. That one she was really happy about. The other was posted from Doctor Malcolm just up the road. That one put an expression on her face like she just read someone had died. She'd put that letter in her pocket and he never saw it again. After his mum left the kitchen to hang out the washing that day, he read the one still open on the kitchen table. It talked about a job offer for her in Broken Hill. From then on, things changed. *'My mum's going to be an important school teacher,'* he'd told his friends. Ben wondered why Doctor Malcolm's letter would come via the post office at that time. He only lived just down the road and saw his mum regularly and always gave that kind of stuff when she was there.

Why wouldn't he just tell her stuff? What's so important he had to write it down anyway?

When Ben asked his mum why Doctor Malcolm had to write her a letter when he lived so close, she deflected the question by saying it wasn't a young man's business again.

Shortly after that bad letter came, Ben heard his mum and dad arguing in hushed whispers for days when they thought he and Sally weren't around. Then, after one of their "no kids allowed" in the kitchen conversations, he heard his mum speaking on the phone to some relatives in Broken Hill. The following morning at 6:00 a.m., they'd been hurried out of bed to help pack up the car for a trip and holiday with Uncle Tom and Aunty Murl in Broken Hill. He remembered looking through the window of their car seeing Doctor Malcolm shaking hands with them on his porch, and then down the road they went.

As his eyelids fluttered shut, just before the ordinary world faded, Ben thought he heard the faintest voice—as though someone had called his name. With the dead of night surrounding him, Ben's head rolled to one side and sleep closed the door on his ordinary world. Breathing the rhythms of a person asleep, somewhere deep in the back of his mind a separate much older spark of consciousness ignited. Quite separate from his ordinary self, it opened a strange and hidden mental passage containing mysterious fragments of memory and emotion unconnected to his present life. He experienced a shift from one place to another in the inky blackness of his deep unconscious mind. He felt sure he heard a heavy door swing open. He passed through it like a drifting ghost and the door closed firmly behind him the moment he was clear. Then, as if he were a diver rising to the surface from the deep, Ben felt the brightness of sunlight saturate him as it drew him upward, and suddenly he felt wide awake. With that came a feeling of buoyancy, a feeling of moving sideways—to some distant place.

For a moment, he felt disoriented and made a futile attempt to turn and retreat, which somehow caused an increase in his velocity away from his point of origin instead. Soon, ahead in the distance, he heard that same whisper again, only now it transformed into a voice clearly calling his name, and with that call he felt some kind of gravity brake being applied. Then he saw a swirl of movement, and the call became louder advancing toward him. Apprehension faded with the onset of a strange warm dizziness, and then he felt a familiarity, like something he remembered from the far past. He had the sense of some formidable obstruction about to bar his way, and then he heard the sound of a great vault door closing and another opening. From endless black to suddenly light of day, he became aware he had arrived, wherever here was. He took a needed deep breath and opened his eyes. All semblance of those lying next to him, inside the aged canvas tent, and the campsite around them, had vanished. Instead, overhead the leafy branches of a tall beech tree sheltered him from a warm sunlight. It filled him as if he were an empty battery in need of recharging. The sun's golden rays filtered through the broad foliage above just as a cool spring breeze tickled the leaves, casting speckled shadows all about. The distant sound of a choir singing some melodious lyric from the far distance caught his attention for the moment. Then he looked skyward beyond the tree, and his mouth fell open in wonder. Gone was the eastern Australian night sky, and in its place hung a magnified celestial vista of a star system. Several of the worlds he saw hung so close that Ben could clearly see craters on the two nearest. The view of the magnified cosmos pressed upon him with such power that for a moment he could only gaze from left to right with his mouth wide open.

All Ben's senses told him he now lay in parkland of some kind, but his memory told him that had to be wrong. Beneath him, he felt a cool, lush bed of well-manicured lawn. A gentle breeze brushed over his face—not a stuffy or stale breath of air anywhere. He felt his body with his hands.

Yep, all here, he thought and then looked left and right.

The gentle rolling slope he lay upon appeared to stretch on into infinity. Many garden beds dotted the undulating landscape as far as he could see. A moment later, the perfume of a million flowers carried on the breeze—a breeze that he also noticed smelled fresher than any air he had ever inhaled. Here and there in the distance, he saw other people of all manner of nationality mixing with other strange beings, young and old. They all appeared so healthy and . . . well, happy. Many of them looked like they were off to a fancy-dress party from the period clothes they wore. Ben propped himself up on one elbow and began to stand.

"Hello," called a young girl from his right.

Ben jumped in surprise and snapped his view around to see who was speaking. There, just out of arms' reach, stood a cute young blonde girl. She had a pale complexion, and seemed about his age.

"How do you do? I'm Lucy Cavanaugh," she said. "Have you seen my mum? I can't find her anywhere."

Her question sounded innocent enough and carried real concern to find her mother who didn't seem to be anywhere close by. Ben frowned, puzzled by her sudden appearance. He stood to speak to her, dusting off his hands. Dirt smudges grubbied her face and the girl's wavy long blonde hair looked ruffled as if she could easily have fallen out of a hay stack.

"Ah, no," he said, looking about. "I just got here . . . wherever here is. Are you okay? You look a bit knocked about."

She said nothing, instead just looked on at him with an odd empty stare. Her fine white cotton dress, quality pink strap shoes, and white socks suggested to Ben she was a girl from some well-to-do family. The pink ribbon, which should have been neatly in place around her head however, looked pulled about hanging down, torn and loose.

"You look like you've taken a fall. Are you sure you're not hurt?" he asked, noticing straw stuck to the hem of her pretty dress now.

Ben looked around for an adult and saw a woman in an important-looking dark business suit and trousers approaching. Her focus was clearly fixed on them both.

"We were at the races," Lucy said drawing his attention. "I went to see the horses in the stables while my mum talked to the man in the pork pie hat before the next race started. I never liked him; he's creepy. Most times, he waits for her in the stables at night. I followed her once. This time he was angry." She began to fidget with worry. "I have to find my mum! Won't you help? Please?"

Ben looked to the woman approaching again.

"Maybe she can help," he said. "Miss, can—"

"Mum didn't see me go, you see," Lucy interrupted. "She'll be so cross when she finds I've wandered off."

Ben wanted to reach out and touch the girl to be sure this wasn't a dream.

"Where is this place?" he asked feeling a sudden real need to see his own parents. "Is the race course nearby?"

Lucy's bottom lip began to quiver. She looked as if she was about to cry.

"I tried to run," she said. "But he was too quick."

"What man?" asked Ben looking around.

The woman he'd been keeping his eye on was nearly within speaking distance.

"I told you. The man with the pork pie hat. He grabbed my arm. It hurt. I don't remember what happened next. Then I woke up here. This is a nice place. I'm not afraid like I was there with him. There's lots of friendly people here, but no one's seen my mum."

The woman in the dark suit walked up to Lucy. She had a kind face, he thought.

"Here you are. Hello, Lucy," the woman said, shooting Ben a glance. "I've come to help you find your way to the rest point."

"Do you know where my mum is?" Lucy asked her. "Her name is Ada Cavanaugh. She's a very important person."

"Yes, Lucy. I know exactly where your mum is. She has been looking for you," the woman said. "She'll join us here soon too. Let's go to meet her, shall we." The woman talked to Lucy as though Ben wasn't even there. "It's just up the hill. Come on. Everything's going to be okay."

Something in her voice seemed comforting, at first, even protective. But underneath her tone, Ben felt she had another agenda. He tried to build the courage to speak up.

"Um, Miss. Excuse me, Miss?"

The woman still paid him no mind at all as she took Lucy's hand. They turned and began to walk away leaving him standing there. Then Lucy stopped after a couple of steps and looked up at the woman. She said something softly and the woman, who nodded, let go of Lucy's hand. Lucy ran back to Ben and extended a closed hand toward him. Cautiously, Ben reached out to accept what she offered.

"Here," she said, and then softly put a small yellow flower in his hand. "Thank you for talking to me. You're a nice boy. What's your name?"

"Ben—Ben Blochentackle."

"Good-bye, Ben Blochentackle. Thank you."

Without another word, Lucy turned and ran to her guide, who led her back up the slope, leaving Ben standing alone. He put the flower in his pocket. Suddenly, as Ben went to call out a thank you in return, he was bowled to the ground. Rolling on his back, his face received a shock of affection via a playful licking. Sitting upright, he raised his hands wanting to see what was climbing all over him, only to grab a handful of fur.

"What the . . . Dogg! Where did you come from?" Ben asked.

There, standing almost on top of him looking straight into his eyes was Mr. Uniss's canine, Dogg. She sprang away and bounced back again, wagging her tail and yapping away. He noticed a well-chewed stick lay on the ground beside her. She snapped it up in her jaws, rattling her head from side to side with a fast wagging tail and a "Grrrrrr." She bounced toward Ben a few steps and away again, enticing him to give chase. When he didn't move she stopped and sat there, staring at him, panting.

"What are you doing here . . . wait, actually, what am I doing here?" he asked Dogg with an inquisitive frown.

Dogg growled playfully, then stood and enticed him to follow her again, running ahead a short distance and back again. Ben stepped forward and followed not really sure what else to do, and just as he became preoccupied with the beginning of a stick-and-chase game with her, from within a cluster of trees, he saw a familiar figure striding up the gentle slope. Showing his big toothy grin and a wave, Uniss came forward, this time without his familiar hat.

"What kind of a dream is this?" Ben mumbled to himself.

Uniss stopped under a single large tree and waved Ben on to join him.

"G'day, mate!" Uniss said. "I see Dogg found ya. Good thing too. This is a pretty big place, even got me sidetracked for a minute. Had to send Dogg to find ya."

Uniss put a hand on the tree trunk next to him. He looked around it as if he might be expecting someone.

"I always liked this place," he said with a grin. "It's nice to see some of the regular folks again and hear about the plans they're making for a new future."

"Are they going somewhere?" asked Ben.

"You might say that," said Uniss.

Ben stood there, puzzled, looking from Dogg to Uniss with an expression shifting toward apprehension.

"Life's a dream, young fella, even the bits we think are real," Uniss said. "I reckon if you're having a dream as beautiful as this, though, friends should be able to enjoy it too! That is, if this is indeed a dream." Uniss looked at the boy squarely. "Whaddaya reckon, Ben?"

His voice had no threat or guile that Ben could sense, and Dogg looked very happy and friendly as she had been at their camp, but something wasn't right. The boy's eyes darted from one to the other. Both of them appeared so real. Everything here did.

"What's the last thing you remember, young fella?"

"I remember being in the tent, and then I guess the dream started. How did you two come to find me?" Ben asked.

Uniss shook his head. "Nah, mate, you came to us, not the other way around! This is our backyard." Uniss gestured toward the horizon. "Do you like it? A lot better than that bloody hot ocean of red dirt you went to sleep in, eh, mate?"

"No, I mean, yes. I mean, why are you in my dream?" Ben asked.

To one side, Dogg rolled on her back, playing and growling, watching the two of them with her legs in the air.

"Well, you could be in my dream now couldn't ya, young fella?" Uniss said. He could see that idea was turning the boys head to soup. "Okay. Let's say for just a minute that Dogg and I are here in *your* dream. You said just before bed you liked the idea of exploring the heavens, right?"

"Ah, yeh."

"Well, whaddaya reckon about what you've seen so far? Why don't you let me show you 'round here a bit? It'll be fun. It's perfectly safe. There's lots of things you won't find anywhere in your world I promise ya that."

From Ben's blind side, Dogg bumped up against his leg playfully. He looked down, relaxed, and smiled at her.

"Well…," Ben said, "it looks a lot nicer here, like you said. Since it's my dream, I guess it won't hurt to look around for a bit. Okay, let's go."

"Good way to look at it. Come on, then," Uniss said and gestured to a wind-swept stone path several yards off to the right.

It meandered away into the distance disappearing through some other trees and shaded areas. They set off and ambled along at a leisurely pace for a while, stopping to throw the stick for Dogg here and there. Uniss explained that the name given to the place was the "Garden of Transitions."

"Exactly where is this place, Mr. Uniss?"

"Well, that's a little hard to explain for now. See Ben, there's many other places like this over distances in the stars impossible to count in numbers. Folks came to these gardens to move on to their next life.

"Their next life?"

"That's right," Uniss said. "This one was built very long ago by some engineers we know as, the Jenaoin. Strictly speaking, the Jenaoin call this place a Transition Bridgeport. A bridgeport is kind of a customs station for lots of different races across the Superverse to move through on both sides of mortal and ethereal existence."

Ben raised an eyebrow. "Both sides? You mean . . . like ghosts?"

Some of the people nearby turned with concerned looks. Uniss gestured for Ben to keep his voice down.

"Not a good term to use here, young fella. Nah, mate. These people are as healthy and alive as you are. The term you used means something much worse than you think it does though. All these folks are just like you, only they've just completed one part of a very long life's journey somewhere else. Now it's their time to go on their next journey. Get my drift?"

"Umm."

"That's alright son. It'll all be clear soon."

After some more walking, they came to a shady cluster of large elm trees. As they passed through and out the other side, Ben saw, spanning away for some considerable distance, a beautiful deep blue lake. Its surface looked like polished glass, except out toward the center where occasionally the water was disturbed by rising dorsal fins of what he thought must be giant whales. At the water's edge near the grass shoreline, clumps of tall rushes dotted the edge. He could see a small jetty with a tiny boat tethered not far from the only dead tree he had seen since being in this place. Swans, egrets, and many other kinds of water birds swam or walked in the shallows, searching for a tantalizing morsel. Not far back from the waterline, directly down in front of them, sat a sturdy white bench, shaded by a huge fig tree. Uniss suggested they sit there for a short rest and a chat.

"The ferryman takes some back across from there," said Uniss.

"Across to where?" asked Ben.

Suddenly, there was a burst of activity near the water's edge and a flock of flamingoes took to the sky.

"This'll be a good place for a spell, I think," he said, sitting down.

As Ben joined him, Dogg rolled on the ground nearby, then stretched out on the grass near Uniss's feet. In apparent doggy euphoria, she dragged her belly along the damp green grass using her front paws, huffing with tongue lolling out the side of her mouth. Ben laughed as she picked up a nearby stick and flipped over on her back with the stick still in her mouth, wiggling like a fish out of water. Once she finished her antics, Dogg flopped on her side, casting her badly chewed stick away.

"She's a great dog, Mr. Uniss," Ben said, smiling at his new canine friend.

"Yeah, she has her moments."

To Ben, Uniss's tone sounded almost like a reprimand to the dog's antics.

Ham.

"Mr. Uniss?"

"Yeah, mate?"

"Do you know what's wrong with my mum?"

Uniss raised an eyebrow looking at the boy. "Now why would you think I would know anything about that?"

"Because I saw the two of you talking when Dad and I went to get wood. She looked a bit upset, like the way she looked when she came back from Dr. Malcolm's."

Perceptive, Uniss thought.

"Don't miss much, do ya, mate?"

Ben shook his head.

"I just notice stuff, that's all. She's sick, isn't she, Mr. Uniss? I've asked Dad, but he won't answer. He always says, 'Not now, son.'"

Ben spoke the last words while deepening his voice to sound like his father. Uniss gave a short laugh patting Ben on the shoulder.

"She'll be fine, I reckon, mate. Sometimes things happen for a reason and sometimes they're random. I think this time it's for a reason. Time is plastic, son.

It sits inside something called the 'Continuum'. That's a kind of cradle that carries everything in existence along, together we call it the Superverse. When you get the gist of its workings, ya learn that time is a kind of fabric, a thing that weaves in and out of everything, like threads in your shirt. Get my drift?"

Ben gave a small nod. "Sort of," and kept looking around as though he was searching for something.

"We never know just how much time we have, Ben. And not all the things that happen are to our liking. But we all have free will, you know. The ability to choose for our self is pivotal to see we get to where we need to be. Don't ever forget that, young feller. It takes a bit of doin' to fix stuff sometimes, but . . ." Uniss paused looking at the boy. "I don't reckon your mum will have much to worry about this time for too much longer. She'll be all right, I promise."

Ben nodded again, then his eyes cut away to focus hard on someone else. He pointed to a woman in a pink pencil skirt, with hat and matching shoes.

"That lady over there doesn't look all right. She looks like she's just been to the races and lost a lot of money with a face like that."

Uniss looked at the woman with some interest. The boy was right. An attractive brunette, in her mid-thirties in an expensive but damaged dress. She had a scowl on her face reflecting someone in the worst of humors as if she'd caught a thief who'd stole her purse. The conversation was just too far away to hear any real detail beyond fragments. It was clear however, that by her manner and the way she pointedly asked one of the people in uniform about whatever was wrong, that she wanted answers quick smart.

"She's got a nasty cut on her left arm, Mr. Uniss," said Ben. "She looks like she's been in an accident or something."

Uniss stared at her too for a short time, then looked back to Ben placing a gentle hand on his shoulder.

"Very observant young fella, you hit the nail on the head. She was indeed at the races, but she lost a bit more than some cash, I'm afraid. Hmmm, didn't like the life tour she booked last time by the looks. Some of you are like that. No matter how much planning and warning that management provides beforehand, most folks inevitably bring back too much baggage when it's time to leave. They can't let go or forgive the mistakes and move on. She's come back way too karma heavy I'd say."

"What do you mean she came back too heavy?" Ben asked. "She looks pretty thin to me."

Uniss heard the question, but didn't respond. Instead, he stared on at the woman in pink for a long moment. Then he noticed Ben switching focus back and forth from him to the woman.

"Do you know what's going on?" Ben asked.

Uniss stepped forward cutting off Ben's line of sight to the goings-on up the slope.

"Well, son," Uniss said hands on hips. "Sometimes when they come back from their last life, they're upset—mostly because they forgot to do or undo something to make things right before they left."

"Come back? What last life?"

Uniss gave Ben a curious look. "All in good time, young fella, all in good time."

Then Uniss turned his attention back to the woman still badgering the individual in uniform. They both watched as the one in uniform seemed to be attempting to reassure the woman with gentle hand gestures and nods of agreement. Then the attendant spoke to her briefly. Moments later, her shoulders slumped and her head dropped in despair. She raised a hanky to her face and started to sob, shaking her head.

"Yep, just as I thought. Maybe she'll come back lighter next time," said Uniss.

Presently, another group of people came along the path. They were led by a man in an identical uniform to the one standing with the woman in pink. The man standing with the woman in pink touched her caringly on the arm and gestured for her to join them, which she did. They all moved off, through a grove of trees nearby just up the slope. Ben looked back to the ground in front, sensing something was missing.

"Mr. Uniss . . . where's Dogg?" he asked, looking around for her.

"Oh, she's trotted off as usual. Probably off annoying someone. She does that," Uniss said, looking around, but seemingly uninterested in her whereabouts.

Then Ben saw Uniss's expression shift to concern. Some of the water birds near the lake started rustling around on the shoreline. When he looked back to ask something, Uniss wasn't on the bench next to him anymore. Ben stood, swinging his view left and then right. Finally, he saw Uniss in the distance, walking at a strong pace up the slope. He approached the same cluster of trees that the small group of people had just walked into and quickly disappeared into the shadows beyond.

"Hey!" Ben shouted. "Mr. Uniss! Where are you going?"

He went to give chase, but in that moment, suddenly felt his shoulder grabbed and . . . just as suddenly sat bolt upright in bed. He looked about bleary eyed. The park was gone, and the tent and campsite had returned. He blinked again and shook his head, trying to come to grips with the dynamic change. Now, instead of the serenity and splendor of the park, the billowing of the green-gray canvas tent walls was his reality again. A determined grip shook him by the shoulder again.

"Ben! Ben! Wake up!" Sally said. "Mum said ya have to get up!"

Frowning, he turned his head to see his sister standing over him.

"What's wrong with you? Hurry up! Mum wants ya to help," she said, pulling the blanket off his legs before running out of the tent.

Ben sat there, holding his face with both hands, muddle-headed.

"What just happened?" he asked himself.

With the fog of sleep clearing from his head, he pulled his shirt on and buttoned it two-thirds up. Outside, he could hear his mother and especially his father engaging in some important campsite task that needed some debate. He got to his feet and pulled on his pants. All the while, his mind went sifting through the strange dream from the night before that hadn't faded at all. He heard his father's voice outside ranting on about something. Pulling the tent door flap back he peered out into the daylight squinting against the bright morning sun. Scratching his head, he went out to answer his mother's call.

***

Though the early summer morning had been quite cool, the heat of the sun had already asserted itself and a blanket of hot dry air enveloped him as he stood looking at his father who appeared to be quite agitated. Albert kept grumbling to himself and rummaged about the camp, looking as though he had lost something important. In the other direction, Ben saw his mother set a pot on the breakfast fire, with Sally nearby. The little girl stood downwind of the low flames, breaking up sticks and tossing them on the fire's edge one scrap at a time. Ben looked around for Dogg and Uniss.

Where are they? he wondered.

But neither could be seen anywhere. It became quickly evident that his father's agitation was directly related to their absence.

"What's wrong, Dad?" he asked.

Albert ignored his question, jabbering on to himself. "I knew I should never have let that bloody pair into the camp. They could have stolen everything and killed us in our sleep."

"Albert Blochentackle!" Margaret snapped. "I'll not have you use such language around the children or make accusations about someone who showed us nothing but kindness with no proof to show."

Albert, turned to face his wife's unusually curt tone. He opened his mouth, intending to snap back at her verbal slap. Instead, he became struck dumb by the clearness of her eyes and newfound strength of her posture. She stood in defiance to his attitude with a presence he had not seen in a year, before she had fallen ill. Deciding to keep his mouth shut, he recommenced his investigations of the campsite.

"Mr. Uniss and his canine friend showed nothing but a gracious spirit to one and all during their time here—to our children especially, I might add," Margaret said.

Albert ignored her.

"Honestly, Albert Blochentackle, your paranoia at times gets my goat! Just because a man gets it in his head to leave earlier than you'd like, that gives you no right to think him a thief."

Albert had always been a light sleeper, and he hadn't heard any vehicles pass in the night that might have afforded the taking on of extra passengers. He'd awoken to find the stranger and his dog absent. Their lack of courtesy to say good-bye sparked his suspicious mind. He looked around the campsite for some clue of any unlawful acts. He glanced back to his wife, who had not changed her stance of protest at all, except her hands had graduated to her hips in annoyance over his belligerent attitude.

"He could have stolen anything, you know!" Albert said. "Wanderers like that take what they can from compassionate people like us. We offered them the benefit of our shade and camp. The least they could have done was say good-bye."

"So, which is it, Sherlock Holmes?" asked Margaret. "Murder in our sleep and carry off the precious water jug, or them saying, 'Sorry, we have to leave early because we have to walk a hundred miles north?' It's going to be a hundred degrees soon Albert, and we have a long way to walk too!"

Albert tightened his jaw and turned from his wife's glare and rebuke, arms folded. He looked around for any evidence supportive of his argument.

"I liked Dogg, Mummy. She liked her tummy rubbed," Sally said, looking up at her mother as Ben approached the pair from behind.

Margaret, in all truth, felt the best she had in a long while. She broke from the displeasure she felt for her husband's unreasonableness and turned to her daughter with a smile.

"I liked Dogg too, sweetie. They were both nice. Ben," Margaret said without looking at her son as she straightened Sally's dress.

"Yes, Mum."

"Take your sister over to the dam and see if Mr. Uniss is there. Watch out for snakes and bull ants, mind you. Mr. Uniss might be having a wash or something there. I'll have breakfast ready for you when you get back. Tell Mr. Uniss he is welcome too."

She made the last instruction louder and more pointed, so Albert would hear.

"Okay, Mum," Ben said.

The two children headed toward the dam. Meanwhile, Albert moved his investigation to their vehicle. Approaching the bus, he first noticed that the vehicle sat squarely on all four wheels with no jack in sight.

"I knew they'd pinch something," he mumbled to himself, then began a more intensive search of the vehicle.

He walked around to the passenger door, then swung it open. Looking inside for signs of pilfering he found . . . nothing missing! Even his pack of Wrigley's chewing gum still sat on the dash where he kept it. He looked in the back-passenger compartment, and there was the jack under the backseat where it should be when not in use. Albert gave a short grunt as his evidence of their evildoing crumbled. He breathed a short sigh of relief, feeling his paranoia subside. Just then, he heard Margaret's voice from the other side of the bus. Looking through the open window, he saw her taking something from the front windshield. From under the wiper, she pulled a note written on an un-crumpled piece of butcher's paper in pencil. Looking at her husband with displeasure, she made a harrumph and read the note aloud:

"Dear Blochentackle Family. Thank you for your kindness. Dogg and I had to get an early start, as it's going to be hot for a walk. I was able to repair the car's problem. It should get you where you need to go. May the heavens watch over you and yours." She looked up and glared at Albert. "With gratitude . . . "Regards, Uniss and . . ."

Margaret pointed to the bottom of the note. Below Uniss's signature, a brownish splotch in the shape of a paw print identified Dogg.

"Now what do you have to say for yourself Albert Blochentackle?" Margaret demanded.

Using better manners than earlier, Albert walked over and took the paper from Margaret's hand. He stared at the note for a short time as the children ran up, puffing.

"They're not down there, Mum!" Ben said.

"Yes, we know that now, sweetie," said Margaret.

"Where are they?" Sally asked, looking around. "Where's Dogg?"

Albert spoke up first, still looking at the paper.

"It seems our guests had to leave early, my dear. And now Dad has to see to fixing the car while you have breakfast," he said, looking across at Margaret with doubt still on his face.

After all, it wasn't likely that a drifter would know his way around the engine bay of an imported piece of German engineering, not really.

"I will see how much our guest was able to 'help' with Dad's car."

Margaret could see that the real reason for his disposition lay in not being able in his view to control his life circumstance yet again. Albert had never quite felt in control of his life. He always felt some divine force had it in for him. Situations like this made the perception worse. Margaret moved a pace toward him and kissed him on the cheek.

"See. Everything's fine now. We are no worse off, are we?" she said, raising an eyebrow. "Today is the first day of a better life."

Albert's shoulders dropped. He looked at the ground and then back up to Margaret's face.

"I'm sorry, dear," he said in a manner that she knew he meant it.

Now with all perception of wrongdoing expunged, Albert looked into his wife's eyes with a clearer head. He frowned, sensing a true distinct change in her.

"You look . . . different, dear. Is everything all right?" he asked, looking at her puzzled.

"Actually, Bear," she said using her affectionate name for him. "It's the best night's sleep I've had in a long time. I feel like something has picked me up and stood me on my feet again." She turned and started for the campfire. "Come on, kids, let's get some breakfast before we have to go."

Soon, breakfast smells of sausages, bacon, eggs, and a strong brew of tea filtered across on a gentle breeze.

There's something calming about a relaxed bush breakfast, Albert thought as he pored over the engine.

He wasted no time in scrutinizing the engine bay for signs of alteration, but none could be seen—except for the fact that the engine bay looked freshly steam-cleaned, and all belts and hoses looked new.

Albert shook his head in wonder. A crack in the distributor cap, he knew, had crippled the engine. He'd seen it plain as daylight yesterday. He had wondered how he would get everyone safely to their destination in the summer heat with Broken Hill so far away.

With a frown, he pulled the distributor cap from its mount that, yesterday, he had left on the passenger floor with some spanners. He examined it closely and looked for the crack that had been clearly present. No sign of any fault existed, nor did any sign of repair for that matter. The cap simply appeared brand new. He marveled at it for a minute and then went to the more important task of seeing if it worked. After clipping it back in place again, he walked around to the driver's side of the bus. He reached in and turned the key in the ignition. The little motor burst to life, ticking over with an easy rhythm and idling beautifully. A smile of surprise broke across his face.

"How did he do that?" Albert muttered.

Then, from behind, he felt a tug on his trouser. Breaking his focus, Albert looked down to see Sally.

"Mum said breakfast's ready, Dad."

Albert's spirits lifted even more. He felt that today just might be a better day after all and looked across to the camp where Margaret had just finished putting the morning meal down on a tablecloth under the gum tree. He looked at his daughter and smiled.

"Yes, it is, munchkin! Come on, we must not keep your mother waiting, must we?"

Sally shook her head. Albert turned off the engine and put the keys in his pocket. He picked up his daughter with a smile and carried her over to where breakfast lay waiting.

After a quick meal, putting the last things in the back of the bus, Albert closed the rear hatch and walked to the driver's side.

"Why did Mr. Uniss have to go, Daddy?" Sally asked from behind him as he sat in the driver's seat.

"Him and Dogg could've come wiff us."

"Oh, Mr. Uniss needed to go in the other direction, munchkin,' said Albert. "So, he had to leave early."

Margaret climbed into her seat beside Albert and closed the door with a firm bump. She looked into the backseat.

"Everybody ready? Broken Hill, here we come!"

"Yeah!" cried the Sally, arms up.

Albert turned the key and the engine's familiar guttural burble brought a smile to everyone's face. He nodded, mumbling, "Finally something's going right."

He put the VW in gear and pressed the throttle. Once more, the engine's increasing dak-dak sound signaled the advance back up onto the road and off to Broken Hill town.

CHAPTER

5

Storm Clouds

The traveling breeze coming through the open window felt good on Margaret's face. As the morning progressed, she felt better and better. The VW bus rumbled along the gravel road at thirty-five miles an hour without falter. No traffic passed them in either direction for miles. An occasional southerly gust struck the side of the bus making sure Albert had both hands firmly on the wheel. Margaret scanned the passing dry landscape in silence. The land in this area was in drought, but there existed a natural strength in it still. Margaret's present view reminded her of her father's oil paintings of the Australian Outback. Occasionally a mob of kangaroos could be seen lying in the tall grasses, just their heads and ears giving them away. Some could be seen grazing not far from the road, always with one sentry standing tall to alert the others about any trouble that might come the mob's way.

Two hours in, Margaret saw a healthy red fox skulking its way across a paddock. She pointed it out to the children. The animal sniffed about, looking for any edible morsel unfortunate enough to scurry across its path. A few miles on, as the VW topped a rise, a goanna waggled across the road in front of them. From head to tail tip, it spanned half the width of the road. Albert slowed the bus to let the reptile pass. The predator disappeared into tussock grass on the other side of the road.

Then, just past journey's midpoint that day, their car ground to a complete stop over a rise on a straight piece of road. Directly in front, a group of fifteen wild camels congregated in the middle of the road. Six of the long-legged hump-backed ships of the desert stood in a tight huddle with heads close together as though in some camel conference. One of them, a large bull, looked over its shoulder toward the intruding VW. The beast made gargling and gurgling sounds that carried easily to all the vehicle occupants' ears. The bull camel bellowed looking in their direction, sounding to the human observers like it was having a damn good laugh at their expense.

"Wow! They're so big and lumpy," Sally said, rubbing her hands together, eyes wide.

"They're not lumps, silly," Ben said. "They have a hump, and some camels even have two. Don't they, Mum?"

"Yes Ben, that's right."

Just then, the big bull broke off from the group and began to walk toward the bus. Albert wound his window up. He reached for the gearshift and thought about putting the vehicle in reverse. But Margaret put her hand on his.

"Wait a minute," she said. "It's just curious."

Everybody sat very still.

"I'm not sure trusting in its good nature is a great idea," Albert said, clearing his throat and hoping his own trepidation wasn't heard in his voice.

"Just don't panic, anyone, he's just curious," said Margaret.

"They're not really carnivorous, are they? I heard one of the men in the pub say they were once,"

"Don't be foolish, dear," Margaret said. "This is a fascinating experience for the children. They are really quite beautiful, aren't they kids? She looked into the backseat. "And did you know . . . explorers have used them out here since not long after Australia was discovered by Captain Cook? See, there, that mangy one on the right. It still has an old bridle on its head. These beasts have been used to cart supplies right across the desert and other roadless places all over the country."

Only yards away now, the bull plodded on toward them, chewing its cud with an indignant look on its face. Its puffy cheeks and untidy clumps of knotty hair on its crown somehow reminded Albert of one of the bad-tempered bricklayers who frequented the pub back in Saint George. He almost smiled with that image in his mind, until it became quickly obvious, to Albert at least, that a bull camel outranked a VW Kombi in muscle, density, and determination all day long. He cleared his throat again and tapped the steering wheel, preparing for the worst.

Margaret, on the other hand, felt completely unruffled by the camel's approach. She felt no fear of the situation and found this new and different experience quite uplifting. The lone four-legged investigator approached the driver's side and with no hesitation dropped its head to gaze inside at the occupants within and licked the window.

"Oh shit," Albert said under his breath.

The camel dwarfed the VW. After examining everyone through the driver's side window, the beast plodded two more large steps forward and stopped. A butt and a huge belly between four legs now blocked the outside view for the people in the car. Sally's window still sat an inch shy of closed. The stench of the camel quickly assaulted their nasal passages, encouraging the children to hold their noses.

"Pew! This camel stinks, Mum," Sally said.

"Can we go, Dad?" Ben said, still holding his nose.

The beast's long neck maneuvered over the top of the VW's roof like a gantry crane shifting to drop a load. Then it leaned hard up against the side of the bus and began to rub against the vehicle vigorously. Margaret grabbed the safety strap overhead. Albert, still focused on the belly of the beast, felt sure he heard her laugh.

"This isn't funny, Margaret!" Albert spat in raising pitch.

He grabbed his driver's door handle, determined not to let the camel in. He felt frightened and angry at the same time, but desperately tried not to show the former. The VW jostled about like a loose road sign in a big wind.

He tried beeping the horn and shouting at it, to no avail, though. He thought Margaret had entered hysteria by the way she now laughed out loud. The kids somehow encouraged by their mother saw the funny side and began to laugh too, increasing Albert's annoyance. Then, there was a solid thump against the side of the bus and roof, which made Sally squeal. The camel's rubbing rhythm increased, jostling everyone around inside like jelly beans in a jar. The roof made crumpling sounds as the creature dropped the weight of its neck on top. Then it bumped and pounded its backside against the front of the driver's door, breaking the side mirror.

"Hey! Get off!" shouted Albert.

The driver's side mirror dangled and clattered against the door, only adding to the cacophony of noise. Albert thumped the horn and the camel suddenly stopped the assault, then farted loudly and gave a gurgle of relief. Margaret, still laughing, got out.

"Hope we stay downwind," she said and walked to the VW's rear and then around to the driver side of the vehicle.

She stood facing the wild beast and raised her arms with a determined yell. The camel lifted its head. Startled and spooked, it turned around on the spot and trotted off. She returned to the front passenger seat and climbed inside to see a flush-faced, angry-looking Albert. She pulled the door shut with a bump and attempted to coax a smile from him.

"We can go now, dear," she said, starting to laugh again.

Albert sat there looking at her with his mixed expression of aghast and surprise.

"Uncle Tom taught me that little move when we lived at the farm," Margaret said matter-of-fact. "It's okay, we have defeated the camel horde." She looked in the back to the children. "Everybody okay? See, all gone."

"Wow, Mum, you beat the camel King! That was great!" Ben said. "Can you teach me how to frighten camels too?"

"Well, when we visit Uncle Tom later, maybe he'll teach you. How about that?"

Watching most of the horde of camels jog away, in Albert's view, the joke the camels had played felt unbearably humiliating. And his father's car would never be the same again. With the silence of the Outback settling upon them once more, the little engine in the back of the VW could still be heard ticking over with clockwork efficiency. Albert sat there with the grumpiest look. Clearly, he didn't get the joke.

Margaret turned to face the front, looking at the road ahead and waiting for her husband to make a decision. Drawing on some kind of pride to do with the preservation of German engineering and family heirlooms, he slid the gear stick into first position. His jaw visibly tightened as he let the clutch out with a jerk. The VW coughed forward toward the two remaining animals standing in the way. As the engine received a belly full of fuel, groaning with a sound akin to an angry wombat, it leapt forward as if it were a huge fat frog, and off they went.

Albert held his foot flat to the floorboard, running through the gears as aggressively as the engine would allow. Much worse for the encounter, the crumpled family transport slowly put distance between them and their camel assailants. The children watched behind as the diminishing group shrank from sight. One sparsely-forested red hill converged with one tussock-riddled flat expanse after another. Each one was crisscrossed by irregular long-forgotten fence lines. The poorly maintained strands of rusty wire, often sagging or broken, spooled back against weathered posts, exposing the paddocks to stray cattle or sheep. Here and there, some old piece of farming machinery—left where it had broken down—showed the struggle between man and Earth out here.

"Barley sugar?" Margaret asked, breaking the moment by holding up a bag of candy.

Sally turned and sat squarely in her seat. She rubbed her suddenly tired eyes, nodding at the prospect of something sweet. Ben leaned forward and took three Barley sugars, and gave one to Sally.

"Thank you," he said, peeling the wrapper and popping it slowly in his mouth.

His mother turned around picked up a newspaper and began to read.

***

Putting the other candy into his top pocket, Ben felt something else there. Frowning in puzzlement, he pulled the mystery item out. There, in his hand lay a yellow Geranium. He felt a cold flush of bewilderment and then a realization come over him.

How can it be?

It looked identical to the one the girl, Lucy, had given him in his dream. He began to go over the events of last night's dream, still indelibly stamped into his memory. Lucy, the grand garden and all the people there, Uniss and Dogg and the things they said and did together . . . the whole thing felt so real.

It couldn't have been real, could it? he thought.

He looked over to the front seat and noticed his mother reading a copy of the Sunday Mirror News Pictorial. She seemed highly focused on one particular story.

"Oh, Albert, this poor woman," Margaret said. "How could anyone do such a thing to somebody?"

"What are you talking about?" Albert asked. "Has your interest in following the tabloids returned too? You haven't read them for months."

"Listen. It's the story about that horrible murder of Ada Cavanaugh."

Ada Cavanaugh? That was…" Ben thought.

"Oh, that," Albert said. "Yes, I remember. Happened just before we left Saint George, didn't it? A barbaric business."

"Says here, a stable hand found her body at the back of some horse stables in Randwick." She paused to read. "Oh my. Listen to this. It says, someone had hurriedly covered her up with straw and a horse rug. And . . . Oh, this is terrible, Albert."

"What is?" he asked, happy for the distraction.

"It says here they found her nine-year-old daughter Lucy, too, not far from her mother's body."

No way. Lucy? Can't be the same ones, Ben thought.

"That poor little girl. It's monstrous," Margaret said.

"There's a picture of both of them from that same day's race, before the murders happened. They're standing next to each other like they don't have a care in the world. Well, at least they had the decency of using a photograph of the poor woman and daughter at their best." Margaret looked to the road ahead. "I always loved seeing newspaper photographs of Mrs. Cavanaugh's pink dresses and hats."

"Pink Dress," said Ben leaning forward to see more detail.

There, as part of an insert for the paper, he saw a color picture of a well-dressed woman in a pink knee-length skirt. She had a broad-brimmed pink hat and horn-rimmed sunglasses, like the ones some of the Hollywood actresses wore in the movies. She looked just like the Cavanaugh woman in last night's dream.

Cripes! That just can't be right, Ben thought staring at the page.

For a moment, he fixed his eyes hard on the page over his mother's shoulder. She went to turn the next page, and Ben went to shoot his hand over the bench seat, but stopped suddenly halfway.

"What's up, sweetie?" Margaret asked, smiling at him.

"I saw her in my dream last night, Mum! She was dressed just like that." He hesitated for a second. "And so was Mr. Uniss and Dogg. They took me to a beautiful park and—"

"That's enough of your wild imagination, young man," Albert said. "That story is about a serious matter. Haven't we just had enough ridiculousness for one morning?"

"But it was—"

"Enough, I said! Now sit back where all good passengers are supposed to be."

Ben slumped back in the seat with a mope and folded his arms, looking out the side window. Albert felt the cold lock of Margaret's glare.

"Why do you always speak to him like that when you are annoyed about something else?" Margaret asked. "After what's just happened, it would be nice to hear about something light and interesting."

"The boy's mind is always off with the fairies," Albert replied, lifting one hand dismissively from the steering wheel. "He is always in some fantasy land, or gazing at the stars, daydreaming."

"He's still a boy, Albert. A good imagination is important!"

Margaret glanced back at her son, who continued to stare out the window.

"Life will not wait for him to sort his daydreams into a useful pile!" Albert said. "He must become more practical. He has to grow up and look at reality. I had to when I was his age."

"Everybody didn't have your life as a boy, Albert," she said, getting huffy.

"All the more important for him to benefit from my experience," Albert said.

"You know, Albert Blochentackle, sometimes you are a real stick in the mud! From something that looked very gloomy yesterday, to everything working out very nicely for everybody thank you very much. It's a very good outcome, including the guest who helped us on our way. From that positive, the best you can do is sulk and find fault. Why? Because somehow Albert wasn't the one in control. We even escaped the furious assault of the itchy camel, and now, heaven forbid the breadth of a child's imagination has you intimidated too. You should run for parliament! You would make a good politician. They are all well practiced at being dissatisfied with what isn't of their own making."

Albert rolled his eyes, sighed, and hunched farther over the steering wheel. The broken side mirror still dangling from his door clattered erratically on the windowsill as they rumbled on down the road. He looked back at his wife, who still had eyes fixed on him with a "Well?" expression on her face. Albert's negative mood finally broke. He realized the lunacy of his behavior and gave a subtle but genuine laugh and nodded.

"Okay."

Then both adults laughed out loud and the kids started too.

"Ben, come on," Margaret said. "Tell us about your dream, sweetie?"

Ben swung his point of view to her.

His mum nodded with a happy smile.

"Are we there yet?" asked Sally. "I'm hungry!"

"Not far now, sweetie," Margaret said. "We'll stop at the general store for some things and an ice cream. What do you think?"

"Yeah!" came the resounding cheer by all.

"Well, come on, Ben!" she said. "It sounded like a good dream. Tell us what happened."

So he did, going into as much detail as he could remember: the beauty of the Garden, the game of stick with Dogg, and all the things that Uniss had told him. He described the lake with all its water birds and the people in uniform that helped the tour groups move from one place to another. He described the woman in pink and showed his mother the picture in her paper that looked like the woman he saw.

"The sun was warm, but not hot like here, Mum, and there was—"

"Okay, son," Albert said. "You described all that very well. But now I can see Broken Hill in the distance and you should sit back and relax a little before we arrive."

Ben sat back, happier now that he at last had the chance to tell someone what happened.

***

Broken Hill had a reputation for being a hard place in environment and an even hardier bunch of inhabitants that lived there. It was nicknamed, 'the Hard Red Country.' The town had started life as a rough mining outland center when silver and then cobalt were discovered nearly a century ago. But it was just as famous for its dust storms and the harsh sun that burned as for the minerals sifted from the ground. The town had suffered a typhoid epidemic in its beginnings, even had its share of turmoil during the Great War of 1914. As a scholar of Australian history, Margaret had studied a lot about this area that her family and relatives had grown up in. She recognized an old sign off the road that identified a piece of history from that time about some sympathizers of the German Reich who attempted to make their mark. Early Broken Hill records had Picnic Flat as the site of the only ground war declared by the enemy on Australian soil to date.

That event involved a group of ore trucks packed with people in a convoy for a picnic day out and two men armed with bolt-action rifles. One man everyone knew as the local ice cream vendor: Goal Muhammad, who always flew the Turkish flag from atop his cart. The other, the local butcher—an Indian Afghani named Mullah Abdullah—was known to all as a quiet and affable immigrant who didn't keep pork in his shop. The two Middle Easterners, apparently feeling sympathetic for the inevitable German invasion, decided to use the road train to demonstrate their allegiance to the Germans. As the trucks of singing day-trippers passed by, the ice cream vendor and the butcher unleashed a barrage of small-arms fire on the convoy. Three vehicle occupants died, and six others were badly injured that day. Margaret's grandfather, George Crebbs, was one of the convoy drivers.

Margaret wound her window down to let more air in. She thought back to her childhood in this area. She could have never foreseen the circular journey that had brought her to accept the job of schoolmistress at Broken Hill Primary before her illness.

Seems somehow right I suppose for things to end where they started, she thought.

She and Albert had often discussed the move and the still-remaining cultural biases against Germans there. Broken Hill wasn't a place for a German to take holidays, let alone live there as they planned to do.

Margaret, though, had argued: "Anyway, those events happened two wars ago and some decades on. By now, people surely would have moved on with their lives, as they should do. Back home, they are hardworking, salt-of-the-earth country folk. They are a warm and compassionate lot once you get past the rough exterior."

The words played back in her head over and over.

Unlikely that anybody there still holds such resentment for Germans or anybody else to do with those times surely. It was another life and time, she thought.

She looked at Albert and knew that, given his own life experiences, he was untrusting. Prison camp had taught him that.

"I hope you are right about all this!" he had said. "The last place anyone should die is in a place with no friends and for something he was not responsible for."

"What's wrong?" asked Albert now, breaking her train of thought.

"Nothing," said Margaret and swung her view to the road ahead.

She didn't agree with his opinion or the self-centered suggestion—after all, she was the one doing the dying at the moment. Before the ugly twist occurred with her health, the final upshot had them agreeing to try things there for a year. If it didn't pan out, they'd head back to St George and start again.

*****

Broken Hill's familiar townscape loomed closer as they traveled into the outskirts along the Silver City Highway. The buildings still remained low-rise, with some roads now sealed and a new service station that had been built since they were last here.

Albert turned the VW onto McCulloch Street to drive past Margaret's new place of work. It looked a tidy and welcoming country school for children. The weatherboard school-house painted in cream yellow with a red corrugated iron roof, had mature trees providing generous shade around the schoolyard. Albert saw it bring a little smile to Margaret's face as they left it behind. Further down the road, they headed toward the train station. Ben blinked his eyes open, stirring in his seat. He stretched his arms up and looked over his mother's shoulder through the windshield.

"Are we there?" he asked. "Gee, Mum, look at the train station. Can we ride on a train, Mum?"

"One day, pet. We have lots of things to do first." Margaret looked over across the road to her right. "There's the general store and Post Office up ahead, love. We could get some things there before we head on to see Uncle Tommy and Aunty Murl, and I've asked for my acceptance papers to be left at the Post Office. They should be there by now."

Albert nodded and slowed the VW. He made a U-turn away from the train station and parked the car out front of the Post Office and general store. He reached forward and turned the engine off. Only then did he relax back, breathing a sigh of relief. Hunching his shoulders to his ears to stretch his neck, he rubbed his face with his hands.

"Made it," he said softly. He looked around outside and then at Margaret. "You go in, dear. I'll sit here for a minute and rest my eyes."

"Okay," she said, then put her hand to the door handle. "Right-o, kids, out on my side, please."

Ben slid open the large passenger door next to him, and both children climbed out onto the sidewalk. Margaret pushed her door ajar. It made a crack and groaning sound in protest to being opened. Just as she placed one foot down on the ground and leaned to leave the car, Albert placed his hand on her arm and she turned to look at him.

"I am sorry for causing the distress earlier. It is not my wish to."

She looked at him with love and placed the tips of her fingers on his lips. Then she leaned back across and kissed him gently on the cheek and wiped a crumb from the corner of his mouth.

"I know, Bear—water under the bridge."

Albert relaxed and dropped his head a little, feeling embarrassed as he began to speak again. "I do love you, you know, and—"

"Come on, Mum! Ice cream'll be melting inside," Ben said, poking his head through the open window.

The moment broken, the two adults felt the typical divide appear when important things that should be said are not. Albert blew a breath through pursed lips, feeling melancholy. Margaret pulled away toward the door and looked across to her son. She reached back, putting her hand on her husband's arm at the same time to let him know she understood.

"Okay, sweetie, I'm coming," she said to Ben, then looked back into Albert's eyes for a moment. "I know you do, cranky Bear."

She pushed the door open wider, stepping onto the boardwalk. Ben took her hand as she closed the door and then she peered back through the window a last time.

"Won't be long," she said with a smile. "Sure I can't get you anything?"

"Maybe a less cynical personality, if there's one in there," Albert said.

"I'll see what they've got."

She tapped the windowsill with the palm of her hand twice before turning away and then she and the two kids stepped off toward the shop entrance. Sally ran forward to pull open the screen door. A little bell tinkled to announce their entry. Margaret glanced back at her husband, whom she saw turned half sideways, resting his head against the door pillar, eyes closed. That picture of the exhausted man sitting inside the crumple-roofed little bus would remain in her memory for the rest of her days.

***

Inside the shop, mounted in the ceiling, a three-blade fan circled overhead slowly in uneven balance. It made a tink-tink sound with some offering of cool moving air that separated the penetrating outside heat. The shop had the dry smell of a very old building, and the eighty-year-old bare floorboards clanked with hollow sounds under their steps. They shuffled by the shelves of canned food and other home sundries to the counter.

"Yes, madam, what can we do for you today?" asked the shopkeeper in a gravelly tone, leaning on the counter next to an old beige cash register.

"Yes, oh, just a minute," said Margaret. "Ben, why don't you and Sal have a look at the ice cream freezer over there? See if there's something you like. Don't open it, mind, just look."

"Yes, Mum," Ben said, then marched off with his sister.

Margaret turned back to the shopkeeper.

"Are there any letters for Margaret Blochentackle, please?"

The shopkeeper, a tall balding man in his late fifties, stood looking at her over the top of a pair of old black-rimmed glasses. Without verbal reply, he nodded and turned away. Clearing his throat through a gray walrus moustache, he scratched the last vestiges of hair on his crown, looking for the latest delivery. From a pigeonhole two shelves up, he pulled an irregular stack of envelopes bound with a brown rubber band. Thumbing through the pile, he isolated one brown envelope broader than the others and slotted the rest back in the box.

"Here's one," he remarked, turning to face Margaret. "'Attention to Mrs. Margaret Blochentackle, Care of Tom Crebbs, Dead Bush Road, Crebbs Station.' That sound right?"

"Yes, it does," said Margaret. He pushed the letter across the counter and Margaret picked it up. "So you would be our new schoolmistress, I take it?"

"Yes, that's right," she replied with a smile.

"Welcome to Broken Hill. Bertrand Wallace at your service," he said, straightening his posture. "I'm the licensed postmaster and owner of the Broken Hill general store these days. Took things over since the brother Alfie died a couple years back. Also, the local council people's advocate."

Margaret thought for a moment while looking at his face. A memory of many years back surfaced. She remembered him, but it was clear he didn't remember her.

"Well, Bertrand, nice to see you again," she said.

Bertrand straightened up when Margaret extended her hand, feeling awkward a woman being so forward. He shot his hand out by reflex before he was conscious it had happened and shook her hand passively. He looked at her a little closer, and then a spark of a memory came to *his* mind.

"Mrs. Blochentackle. Are you from this area?" he asked, looking at her and then over to the two children.

"Yes, I am."

"Right. Town councilor Max Holt mentioned an old local was taking over the vacant School Marm's position."

Margaret smiled. "I see the bush telegraph is still alive and well in Broken Hill, Bertrand."

"It's our fastest form of news, madam. And usually the most colorful, if you catch my drift."

"Yes, Bert, I do. Could I get an ice cream for the kids, please?" she asked, looking around to see where they were.

Bertrand walked over to the freezer and slid the top glass plate back.

"Two of these do?" he asked, pulling out two Paddle Pop ice creams and holding them up for approval.

Margaret nodded. "That will be fine, thanks."

"Here you go, kids," Bertrand said, handing them one each. "You're Cecile Crebbs' daughter, that sound right?"

"Thank you," both the kids said accepting the offering with a smile. Sally held hers up to her mother.

"I am," Margaret said, helping Sally fold the wrapper down on the ice cream.

"Sorry. I didn't recognize you, lass. Last time I saw you, your hair was in pig-tails and you were just a slip of a girl. Your dad, Cess, was a gentleman. Sorry to see him and the missus leave the area. How are he and Maggie doing anyway?"

"They're both well, thanks. Happy to be off the property. Dad doesn't know what to do with himself half the time now, though. A small garden patch hardly compares to what he worked with on the farm every day."

"Hmm, well, give 'em our best when you see 'em next."

"I will. Does Tom Crebbs still come in to check mail on Thursdays?"

"Yep. Regular as clock-work. I'd expect him in here today 'round 2:30 p.m."

"Good. Can you let him know that his niece Marg is in town? We'll be staying with Mrs. Lowry overnight. He can find us there when his business is done."

"Okay, I'll tell him when he comes in. Happy to see locals returning—and congratulations on the new job. The kids will all benefit from your tutelage, I'm sure. I'm a member of the P&C here in town too. So I'll see you at the fundraiser meeting at the end of the month."

Margaret nodded again. "Come on, kids. Dad's in the car waiting. Thanks, Bert, see you again."

Sally walked in front of her mother and brother toward the exit and pushed the screen door wide open. A mask of hot dusty air covered their faces as a blowfly took advantage of the way in. Hurtling close past Ben's face, he pulled back to avoid a collision with the insect's flight path. It sounded like a high-speed miniature speedboat disappearing inside the shop. Margaret, directly behind him, pulled her face back too and then she and Ben followed Sally out onto the boardwalk.

***

Outside, the wide red gravel street looked peaceful. Just as Margaret let the screen door go to clatter shut with the little doorbell tinkling behind, several things happened at once. To their right, across the street, they saw a few of the townsfolk, many wearing hats to fend off the sun, going about their daily business in nearby shops.

Directly in front of them, Ben saw his father peacefully dozing in the VW. His head leaned against the open window and door pillar, his mouth half open. Coming up the road in the short distance from behind their car, two vehicles rumbled along a little faster than the speed limit allowed. The first, a weather-beaten old black Plymouth, had a driver and passenger in the front seat. Close behind it traveled a big old Dodge wool truck covered in Outback red dust. Three rough-looking men in blue shearers' singlets sat across the front seat. Stacked high beyond capacity with large wool bales up front, the rear of the truck had covered stores piled nearly as high. The sound of a deep gurgle from its diesel engine warned of its approach.

As the Plymouth rolled toward them, a feeling of foreboding saturated Ben. He didn't know why, but for him, suddenly all the surroundings seemed to go deathly quiet. The very moment the black car drew parallel with his father's parked VW, the quiet country town street shifted from serenity to something calamitous. Everyone close by—including Albert, who was suddenly jarred awake by the noise of a warning horn—turned their attention to the sound of the black Plymouth's brakes being stabbed hard. Then, from around the Plymouth driver's side of the front bumper, they heard a dog yelp in pain and witnessed it barely miss the passenger-side front wheel. The animal skittered past the nose of the vehicle. It passed in front of the VW toward some witnesses on the boardwalk at full gallop.

"No!" said Ben crying out in fear.

He recognized that canine.

"That's Dogg!"

There was no dog on the other side of the road a second ago, Ben was sure; he'd had a clear view. She'd just come out of nowhere. Sally saw Dogg too, and watched in trepidation as Dogg's back legs barely missed the screeching front wheels by a breath. She screamed with a shrill cry of terror and turned away to her mother, hands covering her face. Ben didn't take his eyes off the scene and instead lurched toward Dogg's approach. His mother grabbed Ben's collar fast, holding him firm. Dogg burst past and vanished around the corner without a look or attention in any other direction.

Everything slowed for Ben as though in heavy gravity. For him, sight and sound churned together, building the force and horror of something far worse about to happen. He snapped his view back to the coming collision stomach knotting with fear. He dropped his ice cream covering his mouth with one hand and winced at the sight of the imminent front-to-back impact of two vehicles desperately trying to stop.

"Shit!"

The driver of the truck fought frantically to avoid the crash but slammed hard into the car's rear. A heavy shattering clap of clashing metal erupted. The transfer of weight and force swung the truck's rear wheels askew with a danger-warning groan of tons of unstable shifting cargo about to fall. There came a huge judder of wheels as the truck's out of control yaw hurled it toward the curb and head-long toward Albert in the parked VW.

Terrified, Albert braced his shoulder against his driver's door. Teeth gritted, he waited to be crushed. Gripping the door handle, knuckles white, he watched the metal behemoth close upon him with dire consequence. In those final seconds, through his open window came an inrush of air carrying the smell of diesel and hot oily fumes that blanketed his face as he prepared to die. A hand's reach from his door, the huge metal bulk of the truck's body made a sudden grinding jerk in a large cloud of dust that engulfed the VW. His view fixed high, Albert shrank at seeing the looming truck and cargo rock precariously over him. A long breath passed as he watched the vehicle settle back onto its wheels with a metallic clatter. Wearing no seat belts, the truck driver and middle passenger had been shunted sideways across the bench seat into the last man. The resulting centrifugal force of the crash had caused a picture of crushed faces in a mixed pile of arms and legs. The last man had hit his door window face-first shattering the glass. His bare arm lay limp outside the broken window, twitching. Inside the cab, no other movement occurred. Boiling radiator water and diesel fumes filled the air. In front of the VW, the wrecked Plymouth's passenger rear door had burst open, and its trunk caved in by the time it came to rest with one back wheel bent. Now flush tight against the curb, its rear sat against the VW's nose —right in front of Margaret and the children.

*****

The pointy-featured male passenger in the Plymouth began to move breaking the silence. He made nonsensical noises that sounded like a mixture of panic and confusion. The driver of the Plymouth, a thickset gent in a dark suit and hat, started to hit his door with his shoulder in an attempt to get out. Witnesses nearby stood frozen, at first, and then two bystanders began moving to the car to help still not knowing what to do next. Margaret and the two children stood on the veranda like dolls looking straight at Albert, who still sat in a cringing posture inside the unharmed cabin.

He seemed for a moment to open his eyes and look toward them. They saw him smile, and then begin to breathe a sigh of relief. In that half of a breath, a straining snapping sound of cargo ropes could be heard.

"Oh God, no!" Margaret said under her breath.

Margaret cast her eyes aloft as other observers gasped too in fear for the trapped man in the VW. On top of the truck's load, and listing badly, one of the massive wool bales had slipped a mooring.

"Albert, Albert get out of there," she shouted, her voice rising with anxiety.

"Stay back from the bus!" someone shouted.

The bale hanging over the bus suddenly shifted again with a groan, as Albert sat there in abject fear, not daring to move an inch. The bale slid further and now hung proud directly over Albert's position seven feet above.

"Albert!" Margaret shouted.

As Margaret and the children looked into Albert's eyes, in the next breath, everyone watched the heavy bale slip slowly free of the last rope and topple sideways. It fell with a horrendous crash right onto the corner of the driver's cabin where Albert sat. The weight of the bale crushed the entire driver's side roof and doorpost before it toppled to the ground. To the witnesses, the outcome felt unbearable, and several had to look away. Margaret felt ill and torn to the core looking upon her husband's broken body from the exposed passenger position. Albert sat lifeless, crushed between the seat and the door. Margaret's heart almost stopped. The only sound heard that drew any other focus was her children screaming and crying.

From all directions, people began to come running to help. With distraught expressions, they rushed to the battered vehicles to aid the injured. Seconds later,

Margaret heard one woman say in a shrill voice, "I think that man in the little bus is dead!"

Margaret stood there, staring like some great hand held her in place. It was all too hard to process. Albert's bloodied form was shocking to look upon. His head and neck bent in an obscenely wrong position off to the side. Margaret thought she felt a tug on her skirt by a small hand and began to look down. Suddenly, she felt her legs give way. Then everything went black.

CHAPTER

6

Everything Changes

Margaret awoke in a hospital bed, drowsy and disoriented. Her head felt terribly heavy, and she didn't open her eyes at first. She could sense that someone else was close by. The sound of a turning page broke the silence. Sleepily, she opened one curious eye, looking to the side of the bed.

In her field of vision, a nurse with a pale freckled face and a short bob of red hair sat, legs crossed, on a chair next to Margaret's bed. Immersed in a popular magazine with scandalous pictures of celebrities on the front cover, she remained unaware of Margaret's return to consciousness.

The room was sparsely furnished, with one empty bed adjacent to her own. On the right side of each bed stood a short steel-gray bedside cabinet. On the opposite wall in the right-hand corner next to a single thick- framed window, bland heavy curtains pulled away in the center permitting sunlight from the outside in.

Margaret could see the last light of the day failing. She scrunched her nose, offended by the scent of carbolic acid and bleach used for cleaning in such places. Un-stimulating walls in off-white with duck-egg blue around the skirting framed an average copy of a Picasso and a picture of Queen Elizabeth II.

The pictures in my dreams offered more life, she thought.

Only a small vase of yellow daises that sat on the little tray at the end of her bed broke the room's colorless effect. Margaret rolled her head to the side with a sigh, and the nurse looked up from her magazine.

"Oh, you're awake, Mrs. Blochentackle," the nurse said in a nasally vocal.

She stood and poured some water in a stubby glass.

"Here you go, drink a little water. Everything's all right now," she said with a well-practiced smile.

Margaret sipped the water with the nurse's assistance and blinked her eyes, trying to focus better. Her head settled back into the pillow. Without any discernible trigger, sudden shocking memories flooded her mindscape. She saw the vivid last moments of the accident. Even the smell of dirty, leaking hot radiator water and diesel harassed her senses. She went to speak, but before she could, the nurse stood and turned away. She pushed the chair into the small side table and then looked across her shoulder to Margaret.

"I'll tell Doctor you are awake," she said, then moved off out the door into the corridor.

Margaret looked up at the high ceiling. Three black flies circled a single dangling light bulb with a strip of yellow flypaper tethered to it. Some minutes passed while she lay there, and her turbulent mind swung from one painful memory to another. The door to her room opened inward, breaking her train of thought. A doctor and the same nurse stepped into the room. They both stopped at the end of Margaret's bed. The doctor, a long-faced clean-shaven man wore thick framed glasses and had two different colored pens clipped to the top pocket of his pressed white doctor's coat. He held a clipboard with some paperwork at his chest.

"Hello, Mrs. Blochentackle. I am Dr. Dougal," he said in a well-educated Australian accent.

Margaret took a breath to look at who she felt presented as a confident man by demeanor and tone. She adjusted her position to get more comfortable and then asked the first questions heaviest on her mind.

"Where are my children? What's happened to my husband?"

Her voice faltered as she tried to sit up further, leaning on one elbow. The nurse standing behind the doctor didn't move to assist, instead just stood staring at Margaret with a gawking expression. The doctor moved around to Margaret's bedside, still clasping the clipboard to his chest.

"Now you just lie back, Mrs. Blochentackle. We will get to all that in good time. Right now, *your* health is our main concern. This has all been a very difficult time for you. We contacted your family physician after someone passed on a letter found on the seat of your motor vehicle that provided an address. When he advised us of your condition, I thought it best to act swiftly. We have put certain procedures into action."

"Procedures?"

Yes, we have you scheduled for a variety of tests."

The doctor explained things with little bed side manner. As she listened, he had her feeling he saw her as just another broken cog in a machine needing repair. Either way, he was in charge, she was just along for the ride, or at least that's the way he made it sound.

"Where are my children?" Margaret repeated more insistently as he went to take a new breath.

"They are fine, Mr. Blochentackle. I'm told that the Postmaster and his wife took them in after the ordeal yesterday."

Margaret frowned. "Yesterday?"

"That's right. You were carried here by a local Aboriginal fellow in a long gray coat. Said he was a friend of the family. He was here until an hour or two ago when I informed him you were stable."

A foggy memory of Uniss talking to her as he carried her into the hospital flashed through her mind.

"Uniss?" she asked.

"Yes, that's the fellow," said Dr. Dougal.

"A whole day! How?" Margaret asked, touching her head, trying to understand the time lapse. "What are you talking about?"

"In town, when you collapsed, I was told you fell and hit your head and hip. So, to be on the safe side, tests—including an X-ray of your hip area—were done while you remained sedated. In the meantime, I called your doctor, Malcolm Reynolds, back in Saint George. He confirmed your medical condition and its severity, describing your metastatic cancer in the left breast and how the disease had spread. According to the records it had emerged recently around the hip area too. He reported it to be quite aggressive."

Margaret slumped visibly, her bottom lip began to quiver, and her face flushed red. She began to cry.

"Six months is the best I had left, Doctor Malcolm said." She spoke softly, eyes full of tears. "Now all this is in my lap too. What did I do to deserve this?"

"Welllll," the doctor replied almost cheerily, pausing to think. "When the X-rays came back, there were some interesting things that didn't match your doctor's descriptions. It seemed the diagnosis was in error, Mrs. Blochentackle."

"What? Error! How?" Margaret asked.

"As I said, the diagnosis that stated you had a metastatic cancer originating in your left breast spreading to your hip area—it was flawed."

"But he told me the specialist was certain. They confirmed it. He showed me the X-rays," Margaret said, looking bewildered.

"I have no doubt your physician was confident about the diagnosis. At first, we thought the problem of our X-ray lay with some poor-quality film. So, I ordered a second, which produced the same result. It appears that somehow your cancer, if it did indeed exist, has miraculously vanished from the last time you saw your physician." The Doctor smiled like he'd made some personal discovery of something unique. "This is an enormous thing to consider, Mrs. Blochentackle, given its implications. Particularly with all the written medical history available about your case. We can find no sign of the cancer at all."

The room fell silent for some moments as the doctor let Margaret take it all in.

"Mrs. Blochentackle, cancer doesn't just vanish."

"But it's gone, right?" Margaret responded, feeling a momentary high.

"In my second conversation with your doctor, he assures me that the cancer was there five days ago. Unless the hand of God pressed upon you favorably between then and now, there is no explanation for your cure. None at all."

A flicker of something Uniss had said at the campfire about better things to come flittered amongst Margaret's thoughts.

"Your doctor insisted the cancer was growing aggressively, and he had advised you to get your affairs in order. Do you remember that?"

Margaret sat blank-faced. Nothing that had taken place in the last two days could be held straight in her mind right now. Then she realized that her cancerous regions did indeed have no more steady deep ache. That constant, nagging painful companion over the last few weeks, was gone.

"We would like to keep you here for a couple more days to ensure you are well enough to go home—and to try to understand this phenomenon," said Dr. Dougal.

Amidst the calamity of thoughts hammering her mind, one absolute point of focus suddenly jumped out. Margaret looked up.

"What about my husband?" Margaret asked. "Albert, where is he?"

The doctor seemed to shrink for a moment and drew a long breath. He looked at Margaret, realizing the woman remained in hope that some miracle might also have saved him too.

Unable to evade the question, he inhaled to speak.

"Mrs. Blochentackle, your husband did not survive the accident. I'm truly sorry; he has passed away."

Margaret burst into tears. There were no thoughts, just tears. The pain of seeing it all happen again, losing Albert, tore her from somewhere so deep inside. She felt inconsolable. It wrenched her heart to shreds, leaving an immeasurable void. After a few moments, she took a few choked breaths and wiped her eyes with a hanky.

"Could I have some time, please?" she asked.

"Of course," replied the Doctor. "Do you need a sedative or anything to help you rest?"

"No, thank you. Just leave me be for a while, please."

With that, the doctor and the nurse left the room, closing the door quietly.

***

After the accident, Ben and Sally were indeed taken to the Postmaster's home which was close by at the back of the general store. That afternoon their uncle, Tom, arrived late to pick them up. Tom Crebbs was a man of the land, but wiser than most about life. It took Tom forty minutes to drive into town after he'd received the horrific news. Being held up with a front flat after picking up a nail, he arrived in town far later than he'd wanted.

Waiting for Tom, Bertrand Wallace stood against the red brick wall outside of his shop's front door. He took a last drag on a Camel cigarette as Tom pulled up with a squeak of brakes in his old Blitz truck. A cloud of red dust wafted past the truck as Tom got out. He shut the door with a deliberate push, and it closed with a thump. Then, adjusting his hat, Tom walked around the nose of the shabby yellow transport, tucking in his flannel shirt into muddy pants. On the ground, he noticed some of the debris left from the earlier collision and slowed in his steps to consider it briefly.

"What a mess," he muttered.

He looked to Bertrand and gave him a nod, stepping up onto the veranda. Bertrand stepped away from the wall and the men shook hands.

"They're in the house, Tom. Sittin' with Elvey. Made 'em comfortable as we could."

"Any news of Marg?" Tom asked cautiously. "I couldn't get through to the hospital at the farm."

"Sorry mate. No, nothin' here."

"Thanks, Bertrand. You caught me just as I was leavin' for town. Got here as fast I could. Caught a bloody flat just before I hit tar out of the property." He shot a dissatisfied glance to his truck. "Jesus bloody Christ. Doesn't this family ever hit a six anymore? How's the kids? Must be pretty shaken up."

"It's tough, mate. A real sad set of events," Bertrand said looking at Tom with compassion. "Happened right in front of 'em."

"Oh gees. That makes it all the worse."

Shaking his head, Tom took a silver clasp cigarette lighter and pack of Tally Ho roll papers from his trouser pocket, along with a packet of Drum tobacco. He wrestled with the packet of tobacco for a bit and stuffed a pinch of the pungent leaf into the cigarette paper and then rolled and lit it. Taking a first drag with his eyes closed, the tip of the cigarette glowed hot. The action seemed to relieve some of his stress. He looked back toward the scene of the accident, and then to the crippled wool truck now parked on the side of the road near the end of the shop. Even from the back, everything about its stance and cargo position looked all wrong.

"I been thinkin' about this on the way in, Bertrand. Best thing I reckon is to take the two youngsters back to the farmhouse with me. Murl and I can take care of 'em till we see Margaret is doing okay again."

Bertrand nodded in agreement. Tom took off his hat and threaded his fingers through an untidy thinning gray head of hair.

"Poor bastard." Tom said, looking at the stained road space again. "Mongrel of a way to go. Albert wasn't a bad fella, once you got to know 'im." Tom shook his head. "Comes at ya bloody sudden when ya time's done, eh, mate?"

"Yep. A bit too sudden for some," Bertrand said as he stepped toward the front door and swung it wide.

The little bell tinkled overhead.

"We best get to it, then," Tom said, dropping his unfinished cigarette on the boardwalk and stepping on it.

He sighed and followed Bertrand inside.

***

Ben and Sally sat in the front sitting room of the house in silence with Mrs. Wallace as Tom Crebbs and Bertrand walked in.

In slumped sadness, cheeks flushed, Ben had his chin planted on his chest, staring at his hands in his lap. Inhaling, he looked up at his uncle. The man that came into his view held his familiar old tan-colored drover's hat in one hand and looked at Ben with kind deep brown eyes. Sally, who would usually have brightened up straight away seeing her uncle, remained miserably somber in her seat, fiddling with the hem of her dress.

Tom stood at the doorway for a moment looking at the two children carefully before speaking.

"G'day, Elvey," Tom finally said to Mrs. Wallace, who sat knitting a jumper in a single-seat armchair close to the children.

"G'day, Tom," she said continuing to knit. "They're a little shaken up."

"Yeh, I see that."

Tom directed his attention to the children fidgeting a little still making his mind up as to what to say first.

"G'day, young Ben and Sally. Crikey! Haven't you two grown up since you were here last!"

Tom crossed the room in a relaxed manner and sat down on the edge of the other lounge chair close to the children.

"It's been two Christmases since I've seen you and yer sister here," he said in his scratchy country drawl. Tom looked across at Elvey, then back to the children. "Your Aunty Murl is lookin' forward to seein' the two of ya,"

He placed his hat down on a side table next to the lounge and sat up straighter in a posture of authority, focusing on Ben. He leaned forward, placing a work-hardened hand on Ben's knee to draw his attention.

"Now look here, young fella. We got work to do, and I need your help."

Ben looked back up at his uncle's wise but rugged features.

"I need you to help me look after your sister till your mum gets back son. I know your hurtin', we all are. You and your sister aren't alone. Sally's needs her big brother right now."

"Where's Mum?" Ben asked with tears in his eyes.

"Yer mum's all right, mate. She's a tough one—always was. She's just over seein' the doctor to make sure everything's okay. Now we got to get you two back for dinner. You must be starvin'. It'll be cold soon too."

"What about Dad?" asked Ben. Tom took a breath, scratched his head, and looked at the boy.

"Ben, I know this is hard to understand, but there's some things we can control, and some we can't. Right now, you can help your sister, she needs her big brother. That, you *can* control. Can you do that, mate? We'll talk about the rest of it later … okay?"

Ben sat silent for a moment, then reached out and took his sister's hand and looked at her.

"Don't worry, Sal. Everything will be okay. Uncle Tom's here now. We have to go with him."

Sally looked from Ben to Tom. "I want Mum!"

She pulled her hand away and rubbed her thighs.

"We'll be goin' ta see yer mum first thing tomorra, luv," Tom said gently. "She's all right, but she's got to rest right now."

Tom stood and Ben followed suit.

"C'mon, Sal, we have to go," Ben said.

He extended his hand again and hesitantly, Sally took it with her eyes still down.

"Thank you, Mrs. Wallace," Ben said, then led his sister past the seated woman, following Tom passed Bertrand through the door. "Thank you, Mr. Wallace."

"You take care you two," said Bertrand waving them goodbye.

***

Outside the shop, they stepped up into Tom's truck's cabin and sat on the big black bench seat. The early night had begun to set in with a bit of a chill in the air by the time they crossed the first judder-bar of Dead Bush Road. Stars filled the sky and a half-moon was already there to illuminate the view of the Broken Hill backcountry by night. By the time they arrived at the Crebbs' farmhouse, the weather had turned cold, gusty, and bleak.

The homestead had once been a part of a huge cattle station. In later years and leaner times, it had been reduced in size substantially to keep the bank happy. The truck's front bumper pushed the spring-loaded gate open and when it swung wide, the truck burbled on through inside the homestead's fenced compound. From the front of the house, a couple of scruffy farm working dogs trotted down the stone steps off the porch, barking to announce their arrival. Tom killed the truck's lights and turned the engine off as they rolled to a halt at the front of the house. He opened the driver's door. The wind gusted through the pines along the fence line across the way with a deep hollow whistle announcing the onset of bad weather. The Crebbs' homestead offered a welcome to any able to navigate the farm property road. It had a high, wide corrugated-iron roof, with deep weatherboard verandas all around to keep the place cool in the mid-summer. Looking through the passenger side window Ben saw that the sandstone pillar supports had recently had some repair and some of the masonry tools still sat to one side of the front door.

They make the place look rather grand, he thought.

It was well protected from the wind and outside elements by a perimeter of large pines growing all along the yard boundary. The front door to the homestead swung open and out walked a short, round-faced woman in a floral dress and white apron.

Aunty Murl.

She stood on the top steps smiling down at them all and Ben's heart lifted a little. Murl had lived all her adult life on this property which had been in the family for two generations. Along with four children of her own, years ago, she'd become Margaret's and her nine siblings surrogate parent when their mother, Marion, fell ill with cancer and died.

"Hi, kids," Murl said in her high-pitched fashion, standing there with hands on her hips and a tea towel clutched in one hand.

"Come on Sal," said Ben.

They climbed out of the truck's cabin. Ben closed the passenger-side door before he took Sally's hand and the steps to greet their aunt. Tom followed on after pulling a travel bag out of the back of the truck's bed and started filling Murl in as he ascended the top step.

"Marg is bein' looked after at the hospital still. Be there for a couple of days apparently. I said we'd go in to see her in the mornin' with the kids."

"Oh dear. Right-o then. Dinner's in the oven," Murl said as she touched Sally gently on the head. "Come on pet, in ya go."

Murl pulled the squeaking screen door open and stepped aside to let the children pass. A whistle of wind in the trees made Ben stop and look to the fence line. There, for just a moment, he was sure he saw a figure in a hat standing in the pine shadows.

"What is it, luv?" asked Murl, looking to see what stopped the lad. Ben looked again, but what he thought he'd seen was gone.

"Nothin' I guess, Aunty Murl," said Ben and led the way inside.

"Okay then, said Murl. "Straight through to the bathroom for a wash before dinner, you two." About to follow them inside she stopped. "Tom! Could you get me a barra load-a wood for the stove, luv? Im runnin' low. I still need to make gravy for the chook."

"Right-oh," said Tom putting the bag just inside the hallway and then left to make his way around the side of the house to get the wood.

***

Inside the house, it was warm and welcoming. Ben and Sally walked down the center hallway taking in the smells of the old homestead. A floral burgundy center runner underfoot was track worn and sat on the original black tar coated floor-boards that were a hundred years old. Overhead hung a couple of simple brass light fittings dangling from black-pinstriped electric cords to light the hallway.

Even though they hadn't been at the house for a few years, Ben still remembered many of the early-century furnishings and smells of the place. He also remembered the fireside stories told by his uncle last time about the farm and its history. The house was built in the 1890s, Tom had told them, by a homesteader called Michel. Shortly after Michel died in a logging accident, Granddad Wallace bought it and the substantial parcel of land that went with it. They passed a collection of family photos from the earliest times on the left wall that showed the long history of the Wallace's and the Crebbs. Ben looked at them as he passed by with a little interest. He swallowed down the lump in his throat though, when he saw a picture of his mother and father when they were much younger.

***

Before serving dinner that evening, Murl saw to it the kids were washed and in clean farm clothes for their stay. Then they all gathered in the dining room. Soon, the Crebbs' children who still lived at home came in from their various day's goings-on to join the meal and the clink of knife and fork began as a

111

satisfying roast chicken dinner commenced. That helped Ben and his sister relax a little and the meal tasted great. Sitting at the large rustic dining table alongside the others, he could see the open fireplace and 110 years of Wallace family history and furniture spread around the room.

Just above a solid oak cabinet against the wall, filled with crystal and all the royal Dalton eating finery, hung a portrait of Granddad Teddy, whose real name was Edward Crebbs. After a suggestion from Murl, Tom told a short story about him tackling a Wombat while they ate dinner which made the mood lighter. No doubt Murl thought it might help take Ben and Sally's mind off their recent trauma. Ben saw a picture of the Queen of England hanging slightly above the picture of Granddad Crebbs. And there were lace doilies on the large burgundy floral fabric lounge, which stretched long across to the other side of the room. The dining table seated fourteen adults. Made from local brush-box timber, it sat solid in the center of the room and looked oddly out of place amongst the other more finely crafted antique furnishings. Well-lit and obvious to any visitor, this space represented the pride of the Crebbs household and offered a homey atmosphere.

They were all a jovial lot, and the atmosphere helped to lighten Ben's heart with some of the banter going on. Sally, on the other hand, remained very quiet. Apart from Ben, the other young man sat at the table that evening was his cousin Evan, who had just started work as a wool classer on another property. The Crebbs children all wanted to know all about their cousins' travels and adventures, attempting to engage Ben in conversation. Talk, though, fell dead at the question of, "Where are Aunty Margaret and Uncle Albert?" asked by the eldest boy who, coming in late, had not heard the news.

Sally dropped her spoon with a clatter, pushed herself off the chair, and went running out the room in tears. Two of the girls went to tend to her, leaving Ben suddenly feeling overwhelmed as well.

"There was an accident today, dear. There are some things to sort out," Murl said slowly.

"So, your cousins are here to visit while your Aunty Marg is being seen to in hospital," Tom said.

"Hospital! What happened?"

"We'll talk about it later, mate. Now finish your meal; it's nearly time for bed."

"What happened?" asked one of the other girls.

Just as Tom was about to say something, Ben spoke up: "Dad died today."

Mouths dropped at the bluntness of the boy's comment, and the three remaining Crebbs kids put their knives and forks down in dismay.

"Well . . . as I said. It's been a very long day," Murl said, standing to begin collecting the dishes. "I think a good night's rest will do everyone the world of good."

One of the girls came back in. Sally was nowhere to be seen.

"She's in the bedroom Mum. Mary's sitting with her."

"Alright then. Ah… you girls help me with the dishes," Murl said. "Evan, you and young Ben go feed the dogs and make sure they have water."

"Yes Mum," replied Even.

Everybody began to go about their allotted tasks, and the evening came to a heavier unwanted close than hoped for.

***

In his bed, Ben stared at the ceiling. Sally, who lay in a bed next to him, had steadily cried herself to sleep. Ben's mind, though, was a cacophony of thoughts and blurred perceptions.

There was a soft knock at the door and it swung open slowly. Murl entered with a glass of hot milk and a gingersnap biscuit on a tray to see a glum-faced Ben showing no sign of wanting to sleep. She sat on the side of the bed and handed him the glass of milk.

"Here you go, mate—fresh from the cow today. Drink it down. It'll help you sleep." She looked at him with a faint smile. "Try not to worry too much, Ben. Everything'll get sorted one way or another, you'll see. Soon all this will be a long way behind."

Ben said nothing in reply, but drank half the glass of milk down. His aunty was right. He was tired after all the day's events, very tired. Murl turned off the bedside lamp and brushed his forehead gently. Then she left, closing the door softly, saying, "See you in the morning."

Ben tried to fight the oncoming sleep for a short while, but soon settled into an exhausted slumber. After a number of abstract short dream vignettes, he found himself in an unfolding shifting dreamscape. In that dream, a sense of foreboding began to gather. A sudden shift saw him standing on the lip of a moss-and-lichen-covered old open stone well. It was the kind farmers used in the time before cars.

Staring into the bottomless hole, he began to feel vertigo and increasingly as though he was being pulled in. Teetering, he felt that he would fall any moment and tried to pull back. But a push from behind made sure he went over the edge and into the inky black. He plunged headfirst with a short-panicked shout, and for a moment, the experience took his breath away as he plummeted downward. With the sensation of falling ever faster, Ben held his arms out in panic and braced himself for the impact. Then the world seemed to tip upside down and hurl him sideways. Everything suddenly slowed with the sound of a great steam locomotive pulling into a station, and then he heard a voice say sharply, "Hey!"

The shock of the voice snatched Ben's breath away as if grabbed by surprise from behind. In the black, he spun round in fright to see who had yelled. Instead of facing somebody close by, Ben found himself face down in the manicured grass of somewhere outdoors. He lifted his head, wiped his face of wet grassy bits and looked about.

"Scrape a bone! Can't be. It's the Garden again," he said to himself and then stood to look for his friends.

CHAPTER

7

The Proposition

The sun felt gentle and warm on Ben's face, and just like before, he saw people of all ages, races and nationalities wandering around or seated in small groups under the shady trees. Some of them looked decidedly *not* human. He certainly hadn't noticed them last time. Most seemed very calm while being spoken to by the attendants he'd seen before."

He looked about to see who it was who had startled him. Nobody stood close by or even attempted to get his attention. Then, sitting under a tall red oak not far away, he noticed a man in a clean white shirt and dark trousers looking at him. He recognized him straight away. Ben stood frozen. He felt his heart pound and his mouth go dry. His eyes grew wider as the contradiction of who he saw struck him, sending his thoughts into a spiral of confusion.

"It's only a dream, it's only a dream," he stammered to himself, trying to hold back the emotions flooding in.

The man sitting under the tree waved at him. A gravity of excitement pulled Ben forward and he broke into a run. As he sprinted toward his target, the man stood with a smile.

"Dad!" Ben shouted, wide-eyed with happiness.

Albert spread his arms to receive his son. Ben ran flat out toward his father and launched himself when he was in arms' reach. Albert caught him, hugging him close. Tears streamed down both faces as Ben held onto his father's neck tightly.

"I saw you dead. I saw you dead in the car!" Ben cried.

"It's okay, son. As you can see, you don't have to worry. I'm all right. It has been a difficult time for all of us."

"He's right. There's light and a way out now for everyone," said another familiar voice from behind.

Ben lifted his tear-soaked face from Albert's shirt and looked around.

"G'day, young fella," Uniss said, touching the brim of his hat. "Didn't mean to startle ya before. Pullin' ya into the Well of Passage that way, I mean. It's important to keep you safe when you make a jump like that. You could have been misplaced."

Ben blinked through his tears. There stood Uniss, smiling, with Dogg, and for a second, he thought Uniss's hat had eyes too that were looking at him. Ben shot a look to his father and back to Uniss.

"This can't be. I thought it was real, but it's not, is it?" Ben asked.

"Not everything is as it seems, young fella. Your father will attest to that, eh, Albert?"

Albert nodded while Uniss stayed focused on the boy.

"I'll explain everything in the right order shortly. Right now, you and your dad need to have a few words." He looked to Albert. "There's not much time, mate. Remember what we agreed." Uniss tapped his Continuum chronograph emphasizing that Albert was on a tight schedule. "The next EM node will open soon. You do what you need to do, just make that transition this time. Best not miss this one, eh?"

"Don't worry. Yes, you are right, Uniss, of course. And thank you." Albert rested a hand on the boy's shoulder standing next to him. "C'mon, son, let's walk for a bit. There are some things I want to say to you."

Off they strolled following the path down toward the lake where they stood overlooking the water. They watched the huge backs of the whale-like creatures breaking the surface navigating the watery unknown.

"This is weird, Dad. I don't understand. I saw you die. I saw the wool bale hit you. Now you're alive and not a scratch. How?"

Albert turned to his son.

"Look, son, there isn't a lot of time. They are waiting for me. I have to move on. I've already been here too long."

He gestured with his eyes off to the distance where one of the uniformed attendants, stood.

"I wouldn't go until I was able to apologize to you."

"For what?" Ben asked, looking into his father's eyes.

Albert took a breath and dropped his head in embarrassment before speaking: "I have to tell you something. Something that I should have told you a long time ago."

"What?"

"You are a good lad, Ben, always were. I am proud of you. My life as your father caused me confusion about many things, mostly myself. A lot of the time, I couldn't get my head straight. It wasn't your fault. I am sorry I never paid you enough attention. I'm sorry for the times I missed having fun together. I thought I was doing the best for the family. In reality, my behavior reflected more of . . . running from the truth of myself. I regret that. It has increased my burden and is something I take with me now."

Ben shook his head as doubt filled his expression.

"No Dad, that's not right . . ."

Albert took him by the shoulders and shook him, looking at Ben squarely.

"Wake up, son! Listen to me! Reality is not always what we would like. But whatever you decide to think, know that existence is far greater than we can ever conceive of in an ordinary body. You can trust Mr. Uniss, Ben. He will be your guide now. He'll tell you about all the things that are important. He can protect you and offer you a great adventure."

"Protect me? From what?"

"Use the courage I know you have in there son," Albert said, touching Ben's chest. "Go with them. Uniss can show you things impossible to know in an ordinary life. Just remember, I love you. I always did. I just wasn't very good at showing it."

Ben saw the tears welling up in his father's eyes. Beyond his father's shoulder, he also saw the attendant starting to walk toward them. Albert's voice drew his attention.

"We'll see each other again, son, okay?

"When?" asked Ben.

"Not for a while. We have known each other before this life, son, in a darker time. It's time to set things right, perhaps for both of us. I know that sounds stupid. It didn't seem right at first when Mr. Uniss told me to try and remember, either. But now my head is . . . clearing. I can remember things. Mr. Uniss assures me I will remember everything soon. He also told me you are vital to helping fix a very big problem he and Dogg have. Oh, here, I want you to have this."

Albert produced a gemstone collar pin similar to the one Uniss had given Ben two days ago. He pinned it on Ben's shirt.

"It will bring you luck just like the pin Mr. Uniss gave you will. So now you have double luck. It's something to remember me by, and it can help you see when there's no light to go by. Don't be afraid, son. It will all be okay. Look after your mother and sister. You're the man of the family now, don't forget. Be true to your heart and always have the courage to walk in an honorable way." Albert pointed to the Heavens. "Look to the stars for inspiration and see as much as you can. We all have potential to do well. Your potential, they tell me, is without end. Use it wisely."

Ben had never heard his father speak that way before. He had such a soothing, knowing tone in his voice now. Albert stood.

"Albert. The EM node will materialize momentarily," said the attendant, now standing quite close by.

Uniss and Dogg headed toward Ben and his father too.

"You have to make that shift now, Albert," Uniss said. "The young fella will be fine with us. We'll take care of him. You have my word."

"Yes, of course," Albert said. "Thank you for allowing me to make this right, at least in some small part."

"All's well and good enough," said Uniss.

Albert stepped back from Ben. "Well, son, be good. Kiss your sister and mother for me."

"Kiss Sal? Can I make it a hug?" Ben said pretending to be put off. Albert ruffled Ben's hair, and they both laughed a bit. With that, he gave Uniss a nod and turned away to follow the attendant up the slope.

"Love you, Dad!" Ben called out.

Albert turned half-about and gave a wave. He then strode on quickly, disappearing through a hedge near the top of the slope. There was a flash just beyond, and in that moment, Ben felt a strange sense of letting go, and his unhappiness, for now at least, faded and he felt at peace.

"Don't worry, young fella," Uniss said. "Your dad'll be fine. We have some things to chat about now too, if you don't mind."

Ben turned to Uniss, who gestured toward a bench that had magically appeared nearby, overlooking the water. They walked over to it and sat down.

"I'm thinkin' you're maybe a bit scared about what's going to happen next. Am I right?" Uniss asked.

"Dreams are supposed to be weird," Ben said, feeling a little more grounded. "That's why they're dreams."

Just then, Dogg dropped a stick at Ben's feet and wagged her tail. Ben thought about all the things his father and Uniss had said in the last short while as he bent down to pick up the stick. He tossed it toward the water and Dogg chassed it.

"Dreams?" Uniss gave Ben a frown. "You still holdin' on to that caper? Get your head in the game, mate. What did you think just transpired here? Tell me something, young fella: when was the last time you remembered the complete order of things in your dreams, while you're still in one? Or, smelled the grass and flowers without having to think about it? Tell me that?"

Now Ben frowned.

"Huh? What does that mean?"

"Do you remember yesterday's events, and all the stuff that happened in order?"

"Well yeah, sure. What a dumb thing to ask."

"You sure?"

"Yes, I'm sure. Can't forget something like that!"

"Okay, fine. Now tell me: in any dream before today, have you ever remembered the details of what happened in the exact order you remember things now? I mean, with all the smells and such, like in this place?"

Uniss gestured to the distance. Ben began to toe the stick Dogg had just dropped at his feet again, still looking out on the lake.

"What clothes was your father wearing just now?"

"Same shirt as last I saw him, but it was clean and he had new pants."

"Good enough, Ben. You have an eye for detail. Not a new shirt, though, are you sure? How do you know?"

"Cause I smelled it when we hugged—it didn't smell new."

"Were his new pants like the ones I've got on now?"

Ben looked down at Uniss's trousers.

"Well, yeah, and that's not the pants you had on when we first met, either."

"Right."

Then Ben realized that the uniformed attendant also had on the exact same pants as Uniss and his father. He also realized his father never wore that kind of fancy suit pants, ever.

"When was the last time you experienced several new things at the same time in a dream, Ben? And then remembered them the next day?"

Ben hesitated. "I . . . don't know."

Doubt began to creep in. Ben went to say something else and his jaw slackened. Fiddling with the pin that Albert had left him moments ago, he pricked himself with an, "Ouch." A spot of blood beaded on the tip of his finger.

"Okay, let's say this is a dream just as you might like," Uniss said, watching Ben rub the tip of his finger.

"Then tomorrow, when you wake up, it should either fade fast or lose its order quickly. Either way, you shouldn't have a wounded finger like you just gave yourself now, yeah?"

Ben looked at his reddened fingertip.

"I suppose."

"Well, what if I told you that tomorrow, you will remember everything? That you'll take that pin back with you to prove you were here? It was something you didn't have when you first arrived this time, was it?"

"No?"

"That pin your father gave just you does not exist in your awake time, does it?"

"No."

"If you still have it in the morning, you'll know you were here. The finger wound from that pin was acquired while you were here as well. Once that's confirmed when you wake up in bed back at the farm, we can get to the real business at hand. Then, a while on when the time is right and you go to sleep again, you'll return here." Uniss leaned in with a grin. "Then, young fella, I'll show you something that will make this visit seem very small indeed, and I guarantee you'll want to see more, a lot more."

"What if, when I come back, this isn't what I want?"

Uniss gave Ben a long hard stare before saying, "Now listen to me, Ben. The next time you come back will be life changing for you one way or another. But

—and I want you to remember this—agree or reject my proposal, and it's a one-way ticket."

Ben felt Dogg put her head on his thigh.

"Once you cross that line," Uniss said, "your life as you know it will be over. By accepting my offer, the heavens will be your playground and an unimagined adventure undertaken across the stars and far beyond will commence."

"And if I decide to stay back home?"

"You will forget everything that's happened here, including me and Dogg. Your life will become a boring egg-and-lettuce salad of events and definitely no adventures like I mentioned along the way. Think of holding a farm gate open for your Aunty Murl for the rest of your life and feeding the chickens. If that's the way you want to go, then we'll shake hands and say goodbye."

Uniss finished his pitch, then waited for the boy's response. Ben looked away and thought for a moment. He tilted his head a little sideways with curiosity emerging on his face.

"Big amazing things, huh?" Ben asked.

"Gigantic," Uniss said with a pinched-lip smile.

Ben stiffened his chin. "Shake on it," he said, extending his hand.

Uniss reached across, casually saying, "Fine and good enough, young friend. It'll be the ride of your life."

As their hands touched, light around Ben began to swirl, making him feel dizzy and he closed his eyes. Everything seemed to fade into the background and he blanked out for a moment. Then suddenly, Ben heard Sally's voice right next to him.

✳✳✳

"Hey, sleepyhead, wake up! We have to go see Mum. Come on!"

Ben's eyes popped open. Straight above him, he saw the ceiling in their room back in Uncle Tom's house. He turned his head sharply to the right and saw Sally's face right in front of him, which gave him a start.

"What time is it?" he asked.

"Time to go," Sally said.

"Cousin Ellen said mister rooster is up and Uncle Tom wants to go see Mum soon. Come on! Hurry up!"

Ben went to sit up, bleary-eyed. He felt something snag his shirt and the sheet underneath. He reached under the covers for the obstruction, and there, he felt a small object. Ben folded the blanket back and took in a sharp breath at what he found. His jaw dropped as he pulled the object into daylight and stared at the pin his father had given him in wonder. At the same time, he felt a small sting in his pointer finger. He looked at it.

"No way!"

There he saw a tiny dried spot of blood on its tip. Uniss's words trickled to the front of his mind.

"Where did you get that?" Sally asked, reaching for the pin. Ben unhooked it and closed his hand around it quickly before throwing back the blankets.

"It's just an old thing I found. It's not important. Come on. We have to go down for breakfast before we see Mum."

Ben stood, pulled on his trousers and long-sleeved shirt, and put the pin in his pocket. Then out into the hall they went and downstairs to breakfast.

***

In her hospital room, Margaret stood in her slippers and pajamas, looking out the window at the grounds.

Another hot dry day, she thought. *But anything is better than recent goings-on.*

She had started to settle a little in herself since the doctor's visit and to process the majority of events that had transpired. While she contemplated the matter further, the doctor walked in to her room again.

"Good morning, Mrs. Blochentackle."

Margaret turned to face the now familiar false smile of Dr. Dougal.

"How are you feeling now?" he asked.

Margaret looked at him for a moment before answering.

"Such a question doesn't have a standard answer for me right now, Doctor."

The doctor raised an eyebrow at the reply and placed the clipboard he carried on the end of her bed.

"Yes, well, I am sure all answers will come in good time. I have had the results of your next X-rays confirmed by phone from the specialist oncologist in Sydney you requested. He confirms what our own tests have said. From the evidence presented, all signs of your cancer are no longer there. I have spoken again to your doctor, and frankly it is a mystery to all of us. However, I guess the best news is you're not going to die." He paused as though a sign of victory should be acknowledged. "In fact, as the case seems to be now, you should be able to live a normal happy life in the future. You must have someone watching over you to be so fortunate. We will need to keep an eye on the situation, though, just in case."

Margaret grimaced at the comment.

"Nothing is normal or fortunate about my recent circumstances, Doctor. I am still to bury a husband, and before that, explain to two young children why their father isn't coming home."

Margaret turned away from him. She went back to her bed, sat, and sipped a glass of water.

"Indeed, and precisely because your circumstances are so unusual, I would like to send you to Sydney for a more thorough examination."

"No," Margaret said. "There isn't going to be any more poking and prodding. I have things to do as soon as can be arranged."

"But, madam, I am sure you don't realize the implications. I—"

"Doctor, whatever has happened," she said, "I have a reprieve. The last thing that is going to happen after I leave this establishment is to become someone's laboratory experiment."

Margaret's tone and determined posture made it plain who was really in charge of the decision.

"You always were a strong-willed one, Marg," said a familiar woman's voice from the door.

Margaret turned her focus to the voice, and her eyes met a cluster of faces peering through the open door. In walked Murl and Tom, followed by seven children—including Ben and Sally, who rushed straight across to their mother for a hug. Margaret felt her heart lighten for the first time when she saw her children. She knelt down arms around them and gave them both a big kiss.

"Thought you might like some friendly faces," Murl said in her normal boisterous, high-pitched manner.

Margaret said nothing at first. She just stared at her aunt while hugging her kids, allowing herself to feel vulnerable for the first time since she'd woken up in the hospital earlier that morning. She stood and gave Murl a huge hug too, saying quietly, "Thank you, Auntie Em. I don't know what I would have done without you and Uncle Tom."

As all the family members closed in around Margaret, the doctor moved to the door. Before leaving, though, he attempted one last overture to get her to see reason: "Ah, Mrs. Blochentackle, I am sorry to interrupt this family reunion, but it's important you know that you could still be at some risk."

All the Crebbs family faces turned to him with concern.

"Mrs. Blochentackle, we are still uncertain as to how such a miraculous recovery happened. Please come back after one month to be sure. We'll speak about this further after you have relaxed with your family for a time."

Standing there looking at the doctor with Ben and Sally by her side, Margaret said, "I'll speak to my own doctor once my children's affairs have been seen to and I'm settled. I'd like to be released today, as soon as that can be arranged, please."

"As you wish. I'll see to your discharge. Good luck to you then," the doctor replied, retreating through the door.

"You'll come stay with us until we can get this sorted, Marg," Murl said.

"Thanks, Auntie Em. We don't want to be any trouble."

"Nonsense," Tom said. "Let's get your things and get you home and comfortable. We can talk about the details later, luv."

***

As the weeks turned into months, everyone slowly settled into moving on to a new life. Except for Ben, who, after his father's funeral, withdrew from wanting most common family interaction. He often isolated himself and could be found down by the old willow with his head stuck in a book of science fiction stories about faraway universes and strange races. Nearly six years of mundane life passed before Uniss returned. When that event happened, it was as Uniss promised, the defining moment that changed Ben's life forever.

CHAPTER

8

Life not as we know it

Ben's birthday had passed a few days ago. The end of another hollow day pressed upon him. His father's last words and those of Uniss never left him and played on his mind to become a burden he had no answer for. The way things were after death, according to the priest at his father's funeral, certainly were at odds with what he'd seen with Albert, Uniss, and Dogg in the Garden of Transitions.

How can they get it so wrong? he often asked himself.

Most of the other young people Ben's age had little connection with him and tended to shun his company because of how different his views on life were. The only person that sparked any affinity for him was a girl his age from school, named Ann Macilvie. Her family owned the local laundry business in Broken Hill. With large, dark almond eyes and wavy long black hair to her waist, Ann was a strong, intuitive, but gentle soul. Her bond with Ben evolved as naturally as sunlight opens a flower; something about her presence always brought a warm stable rhythm to his world. His mum had noticed their friendship too and arranged invitations for Ann to join them for lunch occasionally to encourage Ben to come out of his shell.

When they went on their walks, Ann liked to hear about Ben's dreams and his experiences with Uniss and Dogg who he'd had no trouble in telling her about. She told him time and again: *'Don't worry about the others, Benny. You're destined to do something big with your life. I just know it's true, and I hope I'm there to see it.'*

On the night where destiny took its turn, the clear night sky showed a plethora of blinking stars that could be seen against the light of a half-moon.

"If it takes any longer, I'll be too old to whittle," Ben said aloud to himself sitting on a chair on the front veranda.

With arms folded, thinking about promises made by Uniss, Ben now had doubts any of it would come to pass.

Then he heard the voice of his mother call from inside.

"Ben, time for bed. School tomorrow, sweetheart."

"I should be exploring the universe by now," he said, just loud enough for her to hear.

"Not until after a good night's sleep, dear. Chop chop, time to rest your brain."

He stood with a sigh and made his way inside, then headed toward his room at the back of the house, passing one of his cousins on the way.

"Cheer up, mate," Evan said. "With a face like that, the sky will fall in. Why don't you book a ticket on one of those spaceships you're always readin' about and find a smile to bring back home?"

"Maybe I will," said Ben, entering his room.

He pushed the door shut behind him and lay upon his bed, wanting desperately for some change to come.

In bed, Ben daydreamed of adventures past, fiddling with the stone pin his father had given him in his last dreamscape. When he'd told his mother how his father had given it to him in a dream, Margaret's response was deflating.

'That's nice, dear,' she'd told him. *'Now, could you help set the table?'* She couldn't, however, explain where the pin had come from when he showed it to her, but she implied that he must have found it somewhere and then dreamed that his father gave it to him because of the similarity. Nobody believing him only made him feel worse. He fell into a restless slumber, expecting to wake up feeling the same as the day before—but he didn't.

***

A deep sleep consumed him that night, and dreams began to filter through until one point when his dreaming and reality completely merged and he found himself running through a heavily wooded and misty forest. A sense of urgency filled him as he charged on not sure where he was going. He needed to find something, a place—no, a thing. No, a door! Yes, a door, his instincts screamed.

Ben ran along through damp underbrush and mist, unsure of where he was going. Branches slapped his face as he charged up a mossy slope through a thick beech wood. He burst through a particularly thick cluster of under-growth to see a tiny clearing. In the center of the dimly lit space stood an ancient stone well. He knew that well: The Well of Passage, he thought. As he stepped toward it, his blood ran cold. Not a good idea. He stopped and thought to abort any idea of looking inside. He saw the well shudder. It gave him a fright and he closed his eyes. When he opened them again, Ben found himself standing on top of the well's capstone rim, peering down into its bottomless murky black.

"Ben!" he heard a voice say from its dark heart. "Jump in! We have to hurry."

Ben felt afraid and tried to back away.

"Come on, Ben! We have to hurry!" called the voice again.

Then, as though someone had grabbed the front of his shirt with a jerk, he was pulled in and plummeted headfirst into the blackness. He instinctively tucked himself into a ball, feeling his velocity increase more and more. He thought for a moment he might turn into a burning comet. His movement sounded like a jet stream and it had that foreboding sense of him soon striking some unforgiving bottom. Ben cringed and waited for the crash. But, just as before, there came the loud clear call of Uniss's voice that spun him round.

"Hey, Ben. Sit up, mate! Let's go, adventure beckons."

Ben blinked his eyes open, and he saw he'd landed in the Garden of Transitions again.

He turned and saw Uniss and Dogg walking toward him. He stood to face them as his vision cleared.

"Wow! It is you. Where's Dad?" Ben asked hoping he might be there.

"He's gone to do other things like he told you, mate."

Ben shook his head. "Dad! Dad–"

"Now that'll be enough of that," Uniss said, then stepped forward, putting a hand on the young man's shoulder.

Ben shrugged it off.

"This isn't right. Dad said he'd see me again. You said you would be back soon. Neither has happened. It's been years."

"Time in different places, especially different dimensions, varies greatly, young fella. Hours or days in some places can mean years or even centuries in others. Now listen. Come and sit down with me for a minute. Helping us get important things out of the way first will ensure you get to see your father quicker than your present notion."

Dogg gave Ben a nudge toward the seat overlooking the lake, the same bench they used last time. Wearily, Ben walked with them and sat down. The water on the lake could be heard lapping the shore. Finally, Ben sighed, looking at the ground.

"Dad said I should trust you, but I wonder if I should be scared of you, Mr. Uniss?"

Uniss sat back and frowned.

"Scared? Of me? Ha. Only thing anyone has to be scared of son is themselves, here at least. Work for the greater good and the Superverse will pay you in kind—that's fact. Trouble is, most recarns never want to be responsible for debts accrued each cycle when it's time to pay the boatman."

Uniss finished his words by throwing a small stone into the water's edge. It landed with a plonk! Then, looking out to the center of the lake, he said, "Look, mate, not everything is as it appears. Many are far too quick to judge what they think they see or hear, only to come up way short of the reality. It happens everywhere, not just in your world."

"And just where am I, then?" Ben asked. "This is in the middle of some dumb nowhere place that started in the middle of a dream and then it all faded to nothing—until here you are again. Nothing works right for me. I never fit in anywhere or feel comfortable in my own skin."

"There are reasons for that, young fella," said Uniss. "And that's connected to reasons for why we are here." Uniss sat up and nodded at Ben with a sterner look. "Okay, you've had a tough run, I'll grant you that—and you have an uncertain road to come. But like I said, not everything is as it seems and you haven't committed to anything yet to find out different. We are here out of mutual benefit. You made a wish—a wish to go to the stars. Do you still want that?"

"Well, I don't want to stay where I am and who I am, that's for sure." Ben said.

Uniss smiled.

"Have you thought hard about what we last spoke of? Are you ready for a true adventure and no way back?"

"Gee, I've only had years to think about it. Hmm . . . of course I am! I don't exactly have a bright future on the farm."

Frowning, Uniss removed his hat and set it on the bench beside him, revealing his head of thick curly black hair. Dogg stood there, wagging her tail as though something was about to begin.

Uniss rose and walked forward a few steps.

"As I said, nothing is as it seems, Ben."

He raised his right arm slowly, pointing into the distance. Then, with a powerful motion, he wiped his hand across the visual space in front of them, like pulling a curtain across a huge window. A sound of cracking thunder preceded a crisp wind. The previously glassy surface of the lake became choppy, forming small white peaks. Then the water birds near the shoreline exploded into the air from the trees and rushes. Just as quickly as the blast of wind came and all birds were on the wing, the lake and all the scenery in front of them lifted, tilting vertical, like some great living canvas. For a moment, the world stood on its ear as earth met sky. Ben's mouth gaped at the wonder of it. Before him, the lake and all the landscape dissolved, replaced with a vista of the heavens. He thought for a moment that Uniss had somehow reached out and pulled the cosmos in, with the stars now so close that Ben thought they could be touched by hand.

The whole event, stupefied him. Now, it seemed he had a keyhole view of the universe, looking through to somewhere unknown. Uniss pointed to the middle view. There, among the vista of stars and deep space, a blue planet with large land masses and cloud layers rotated. It appeared to be drawing closer. Looking at it was like watching the worlds Ben had seen in science fiction movies at the theater.

Is that . . . Earth? he wondered.

With mouth ajar and eyes popped wide, Ben swung his point of view from the planet to Uniss and back again.

"But wait, there's more," Uniss said, before sitting down beside him again.

Uniss checked his Continuum chronograph and gave Ben a wink. He placed a hand on the boy's shoulder.

"Good enough," said Uniss. He raised a hand and touched the back of his ear. "We're good to go Central."

A second later, everything around them—apart from the bench they sat on—dissolved, leaving them suspended in space on the park bench. Ben grabbed the edge of the seat in fright, his knuckles turning white while Dogg walked about in front, tongue lolling about—walking on nothing. She trotted around to the side of the seat and licked Ben's hands.

"No. Not Earth. Like I said, young fella, nothing is as it seems. Don't worry, you're quite safe. This is where your adventure begins. In front of you is the planet Tora. It's an interesting place—dangerous, but interesting. Lots of strange things not found where you come from down there, and a ton more mystery beside. That's where we're headed, Ben. Time to sign up or go home, mate."

"How dangerous?" Ben asked, eyes darting from the planet to Uniss.

"Whoever heard of a safe adventure, mate? This is the door. It's about to close. We can put everything back, as it was—not including your father, of course, as that's gone too far. You'll go on growin' up and havin' the same ordinary life with not much to worry about. If we part company now, this will only ever be remembered as a fading dream, and then you'll forget all of it completely."

"I don't want that," said Ben.

"Then come with us. See things they haven't even written about in fantasy novels on your world. You'll learn stuff, know stuff, stuff that nobody else will know back home. You will be counted as someone special with us, with responsibilities. Where we come from, you'll be respected as a one who made his mark."

Uniss stood and took a couple of steps across the nothingness and turned to look at Ben.

"Be clear. Once we agree today, it's not reversible—ever! Many things that might have been, will never be. Things will be very different when you go back to Earth for a visit, if it can be arranged."

Ben went to speak, but Uniss raised a finger, his voice powering on.

"And you'll have to think on your feet, a lot, and do exactly what you're told when you're told. Can you do that, Ben?"

"Are you sure I'll get to see my family again?"

"Like I said, young fella, anything is possible, most of the time," Uniss said with a grin.

"You won't regret it, Ben, we'll look after you," Dogg said.

Ben felt like his eyes were about to pop out of his head.

"You . . . You can talk! Now I am going nuts."

Dogg wheezed out what sounded like a laugh.

"Don't be silly, dear boy. Of course I can talk. I just haven't had anything to say, until now. Come with us, Ben, as Uniss said, you won't regret it. We'll protect you always."

Ben sat there, musing over their proposal.

What about Mum and Sal? Dad told me to look after them, he asked himself.

"Whenever you go back to see them, they won't ever know you've been away. That's how things work," Dogg said. "However, unlike for you, time and evolution for them trudges on at a normal mortal rate. They will get older, and in their experience, so too will you. With the knowledge you gain, you will be able to help them in ways impossible with an ordinary life."

Ben sat for a moment, twiddling his thumbs, chin down, in thought.

"Okay," he said finally. "Maybe going with you will help me find an answer."

"To what, Ben?" asked Dogg.

"To where I fit," said Ben.

"Excellent!" Uniss said. "Here, just so it's official, sign this."

Uniss produced a small tablet from his top pocket. It had a luminous screen. He handed Ben an eagle-feather quill with a gold nib.

"This looks official. Where's the ink?" Ben asked.

"Oh, it is. Don't worry about that," Uniss said. "Just sign your name on the screen."

Ben pressed the nib of the quill on the tablet. He signed his name and watched it appear on the smooth white face. As soon as Ben finished his signature, Uniss took the quill and tablet back.

"Great, mate."

Then Uniss slid it neatly back into his top pocket with a nod, giving his pocket a pat.

"Okay," Uniss said. "That's done, you're in. Listen up. The planet we are about to step on to is called Tora by the locals for a reason. It's their common tongue meaning for 'to engage.' Atmosphere and gravity are much the same as Earth, with a couple of exceptions that you'll see shortly. There are continents with forests and deserts, and mountains—both volcanic and snowcapped. It has deep oceans and there is an abundance of different forms of sentient life, both mortal *and* ethereal. The difference starts there. There are civilizations and micro-cultures of considerable diversity. We will be interested primarily in two of those."

"What's a sen-she-ant again?"

"Sentient," Uniss corrected. "It's a lifeform that's recognizes its own individual consciousness and is able to reincarnate—to evolve into something greater. It is something that's able to know it is separate from all the other base elements . . . like you know you are you."

"So, what's an ethereal then?"

A curl of a smile lifted on Uniss's lip and he patted Ben on the shoulder.

"That we'll cover later." Uniss pointed at Tora. "Down there, on Tora, we cannot be seen or heard, for the most part—except if we interfere with one of the locals by physical contact or impacting on their personal Continuum timelines. So that means no talking to or touching anyone deliberately. Look, don't touch. Clear so far, young fella?"

Ben nodded.

"Next, remember: at first sign of the enemy, do nothing. That means no matter how bad things get around you, if you take no action to get yourself involved, you cannot be harmed or made part of the events happening there, okay?"

Ben looked at him, feeling puzzled.

"If I'm already there, aren't I interfering anyway?"

"Not while you are tethered to us. You're off the grid now son. You're workin' with Wardens of the Intercosmos. We exist on a different frequency to the locals; so long as you don't interfere, no harm done.

"Okay," Ben said.

"Lastly, you can speak or think to either of us anytime without fear of other ramifications. Your mind is a much stronger transmitter than your mouth, Ben. It can stretch across worlds if you know how to project it. Some people on your world have a partial ability left over from other incarnations. Thoughts in people are like radio waves, Ben. They can be received by anyone with the right antenna. Some are better receivers than others. I'm open—or rather, now tuned into—your thoughts all the time, so is Dogg. It's for your safety when we travel and so is that lucky pin I gave you."

Ben examined the pin Uniss had given him with deeper interest.

Knew it was special. "So, I can't get up to stuff without you guys knowing what I'm doing?" asked Ben.

"We can only read your thoughts if you accept that it's okay," Uniss said.

"But what if I don't want you to?"

"Then it's forbidden by the Council of Evercycles. They are the ones responsible for all creation, and we are bound by their law. But it would make our job down there difficult and more dangerous if we didn't have that communication with you."

Ben looked over to Dogg and shook his head, still in disbelief.

"Okay, I get it—I think. We can talk mind to mind, right?" Ben said.

"Right," said Uniss.

"That's so mad," said Ben.

"So is Dogg like you—I mean . . . Scrape a bone! I thought she only ever said Woof, until she spoke a minute ago. I knew she was smart, but I never dreamed she is all this." Ben looked at her. "Hope I didn't cause any offense— you know, with canine remarks.

"None at all," said Dogg.

"So, is she like you, Uniss?"

Uniss chuckled while Dogg walked over closer to Ben.

"I'm such a whole lot more than he is!" she said in her mature queen-of- England's best English.

"Lesson One, Apprentice, it's always in the eyes. The eyes are the window to the soul. As Uniss told you, not all is as it seems in the Superverse."

Ben sighed, nodded and turned back to Uniss. He thought for a moment. "Okay, well, then . . . I suppose it's all right, then."

"Excellent," Uniss said in a cool tone. "Here, just so it's official, sign here."

Uniss presented Ben the tablet again and passed him the gold-tipped quill to sign his name once more. As quickly as Ben finished, Uniss took back the quill and tablet.

"Can we try it?" Ben asked.

"Try what?" Uniss asked.

"You know, talking mind to mind," Ben said.

"Ah, okay, *how's this?*" Uniss said within Ben's mind.

"Whoa . . ." Ben said aloud.

"No, mate. Think it. say it in your mind," Uniss said mentally.

"Uh . . . Okay . . . how? *Um, like this? Am I doing it right? Do you hear me?*"

"You don't have to shout mate. You're comin' in loud and clear."

"Yes, he is," Dogg said chiming in.

"Whoa . . . group chats," Ben said. *"How cool would it be if everyone could do this! But it does feel weird,"*

"Only the first few times, then it's like breathing," Uniss said aloud. "Okay, let's take a walk on the wild side starting with a trip to the Ludd continent, young Ben, Adventurer Apprentice Warden of Earth."

Ben grinned at the name.

"Hold my hand, young fella, and don't let go."

The moment Ben gripped Uniss's hand, he felt as though he'd been shot out of a cannon toward the planet. Or was the planet being flung toward them? He never did figure that out.

Then, like sherbet in water, he felt himself dissolve and be swept away by some divine wind.

CHAPTER

9

Along Came a Scarzen

Three silver shafts of light spilled onto the sparsely forested midlands of the Toran continent called Ludd. As Uniss, Dogg, and Ben materialized, the first things Ben saw would stay with him for the rest of his days. When his vision cleared from being transported in a manner he had no words for, his first view defied a modern Earth lad's explanation. Standing beside Uniss, he scanned from left to right in amazement. His gaze froze at half a head turn to the right with a cornfield stretching away for miles. But it was the massive jet-black stone fortress structure opposite that set his heart pumping.

"What is that?" asked Ben.

Uniss checked his Continuum chronograph ignoring the question. "Good enough," he said to himself. "Feel it, Dogg?"

"I do," she said, standing on his left.

Uniss looked at Ben.

"Welcome to planet Tora and the continent of Ludd's wild center, son. Specifically, welcome to Scarza, home territory to the toughest kick-arse warrior race to be created below god status. What did I tell ya? Pretty spectacular, huh?"

The structure in front was so vast in construction that it took Ben several breaths to accept what he saw. The shiny concave black stone wall that stretched for miles stood with a clear purpose of warning. It was built so massive that Ben thought it must have been made by giants.

"The walls must be fifty feet high," Ben said.

"Ninety-five, by your measurement actually," said Uniss. "To the parapet across the front anyway, and fifty more up the sides into the foot of the mountain behind. Some of the bunker's blocks weigh a hundred and fifty ton, each." Uniss bent to whisper in Ben's ear. "And none of it made using the wheel."

"Struth. How can they do that? I can't see a seam or join anywhere."

"No, and you won't either," said Dogg.

It looked like something from an Earth Dark Ages fantasy novel, only engineered with a precision and masonry skill unrivaled anywhere.

"Looks like a one-piece sculpture popping from the foot of that mountain range directly behind," said Ben.

"Its front wall stretches for miles in both directions," said Uniss.

Uniss crouched and Ben did the same as Dogg walked up on his left.

"The glass-stone Scarzen use for construction comes from those mountains and can be polished to a mirror finish. It a bit like Obsidian on Earth. That's why Scarzen bunker walls gleam that way. At first glance, the sloping front walls seem a flaw in the defense, but the stone is incredibly tough and slippery when oil is spread down the surface."

Ben nodded. "I saw the ocean once back home, and those front walls remind me of the big dumping waves."

"You're right there, young fella. The overshot lip at the top of the wall stops enemy grappling hooks and such from getting hold. As a part of general defense, the Scarzen use a rolling-fire strategy."

"Rolling Fire?"

"If they are ever besieged, they use a barrage of big woven cane balls stuffed with cornhusks from these fields nearby that have been soaked with a paraffin oil. Hundreds of them are lit on the ramparts and rolled down the stone slopes. When they bounce and hit the open trench there at the bottom, it makes a hell of a firestorm. The wind currents created push the flames away from the bunker and into the fields here. The flammable oil and packed dry cornhusks burn ferociously hot."

"So, they are serious about winning the battle," said Ben.

"No Scarzen bunker has ever been breached. No matter how many times I come back here, it's still an impressive sight." Uniss looked at Ben. "And it's inside those walls we are going to investigate. Over that way," said Uniss pointing.

To Ben's right, some way off, the outline of two massive studded gates stood.

"Can you hear it?" Uniss asked.

Listening hard, Ben heard on the soft breeze fragments of sound from beyond the walls. Studying the fortress again, he saw that, just visible beyond the top of the wall's curved leading edge, about every forty feet apart, stood some kind of black domed tower. Each had vertical narrow openings like the old castle murder holes that Ben had seen in some of his mum's history books. Suddenly, Ben caught a glimpse of gray figures moving now and then near the round domes.

"I see guards, Mr. Uniss," said Ben.

"That you do, young fella," said Uniss. "Now remember: talk to me or Dogg only, whether aloud or in your head."

"I'm a bit nervous," said Ben.

"Good, then you'll pay attention," said Uniss. "Just do what I tell you and there'll be no problems."

"Okay."

"If you do break this law and communicate in any way with mortals here, your presence will be noted by them and everyone else in ear and eye shot immediately—which would be . . . awkward for everyone. If that ever happens, you run—don't think. Ya run! Run until you can be out of sight."

Ben nodded, eyes wide.

"Like falling dominoes, Ben, once an individual sees you and alerts another, everyone else in line of sight will see you too and they'll all come for you. You must be out of sight and more than seven feet away from them for twelve seconds to pass, then the 'dissolve' will take effect and you will be invisible to them once more."

Uniss looked critically at Ben's attire.

"Hmm, that won't do."

Ben looked down and realized that he was still clad in his bedclothes.

"Not good travel gear for Scarza, mate. We better do something about that," Uniss said. "If those inside were to see you this way, they'd mistake you for one of a race that are their sworn enemy and worth killin' proper. Let's get you into some more functional duds."

Uniss ran his palms down the boy's arms and legs. As he did, Ben's clothing transformed into a long-sleeved cotton shirt and sturdy pair of trousers, similar to his new mentor's own style.

"You better put these on too," said Dogg.

Ben looked to her feet to see a pair of black shin-length combat style leather boots. He sat to pull them on for a perfect fit.

"That'll do for now," Uniss said. "Remember, mate, you're not ethereal. You can't walk through walls.

If you jump off a high one, it will hurt, a lot. Keep to the rules and you won't become anyone's next bag of fertilizer, okay?"

"Okay.'

 Uniss looked to Dogg. "You've got stuff to do."

"That job up north we spoke about, in Flaxon territory—see what's come of Regent Trabonus's meddling. What he intends will give Starlin and Herrex just the break they need. Don't want a repeat of last time. We don't know what Starlin intends just now, but it won't be for the good of any in residence here, that's certain."

"Tra-who?" Ben asked.

"A little wannabe emperor who's poking his fingers in places that could get a lot of people burned," said Uniss. "Right, Dogg, let's get to it."

Dogg trotted off, disappearing into the mature cornfield.

Uniss turned toward the direction of the gates in the distance.

"Follow me, and stay sharp!" Uniss said, walking toward the fortress gates, "The Scarzen are just about the most incredible sentient that the pattern-makers ever produced for the Evercycle Council, as far as close-quarter mortal combat and kinetic capability that is."

"Pattern Makers?"

Uniss glanced at his young apprentice.

"Pattern-makers—those whose responsibility it is to develop, research, and optimize all approved sentient designs passed by the Evercycle Council. There's only one other race aside from the Scarzen that can come near to that claim in close combat, and that's a race called the Tengu, who fortunately are not part of this world. The Scarzen are isolated on this planet with no permission given to have the capability of off world evolution—yet." Uniss stopped and examined a group of figures approaching the front gates from the opposite direction. "Okay, see that merchant train about to enter the bunker through the main gate?"

Uniss looked left, to see Ben's steps lagging behind still being distracted by the scene of the bunker.

"Hey, you listening?"

"Yes, sir," Ben said, spurred back to full attention.

"Those things they're ridin' and leading are big as African Elephants," said Ben.

"They're called Drommal, kind of a cross between an Earth's prehistoric long-haired rhinoceros and an American Bison, if that was possible. The Scarzen use them for cavalry."

"Cripes, how big are the Scarzen?"

"They are impressive. You'll see. At an average of five tons each, a Drommal make a hell of a frontline charger."

"The red gates look like Ogres built them to keep dragons out with all those big gold knobs and metal plates," said Ben.

"No dragons on this world, mate. Life's too cutthroat here for them. Come on, stick close. We'll follow them inside."

Ben grabbed Uniss's sleeve, giving it a light tug as they marched forward hearing the bunker's great hinges creak as the gates swung open.

"Mr. Uniss . . . why are there two statues of what looks like Dogg on either side of the gates?" Ben asked with a frown.

"Oh, that. Well . . . now, mate. It just looks like Dogg, that's all. The Scarzen like dogs—a lot. They've kinda . . . kinda been together for a long time in Scarzen history, you might say."

"But, Uniss, that's Dogg—our Dogg! There's even the bit missing off the statue's right ear, see? Just like she's got."

Ben pointed at the obvious misshapen ear tip on the twelve-foot high statue closest as they approached the gates. Close by a small crowd of tall Bedouin-looking characters waited to go in.

"Well, there's a bit of a likeness, I'll agree. Thought they'd forget about all that by now," Uniss mumbled under his breath. He hustled Ben toward the drommal train, where flies hung around the lumbering beasts head and backside. "Look, mate, we'll talk about that later, okay? Come on, or we'll miss our chance."

The travelers in colorful robes stood beside their beasts of burden speaking and using gesticulations with a language that sounded to Ben like a cluster of guttural urges.

"What are they saying, Uniss?" Ben asked.

"Eh? You should be able to understand them with your—oh, crikey! I clean forgot to give you this."

Uniss fished a tiny object out of his pocket and held it up for Ben to see.

"It's a universal translator. With this little thing, you'll be able to understand just about any language you encounter here. Here you go."

Ben saw that the wafer-thin device matched the color of his own skin. He felt Uniss push it in behind his left ear.

"That'll do nicely. Go ahead and see if it's working."

Uniss waved a hand toward the merchants.

Ben looked that way and focused his attention on the travelers' voices.

"Sounds like they're complaining about being on the road for so long their feet and Coloids hurt, whatever they are—and wanting to get something to eat."

"Yep. Sounds the same to me, so you're all set now."

Ben looked back to the travelers. Behind the main group waited a smaller merchant train using animals that could easily have been a cousin to a camel, only they had two humps that sat left and right of the spine of the beast. One of the drommal close to Ben farted and he walked quickly around the other side of Uniss.

"Man! I thought our camels stank!"

Cupping his hand to his nose, he tried to get away from the stench. Sounds of activity from inside the bunker suddenly became more audible as another set of inner gates some yards inside the entrance swung inward with a heavy creak.

"Hope it smells better inside, Mr. Uniss," Ben said.

"Just 'Uniss' mate—no title necessary when we're on the road. Okay, you just heard me mention an individual called 'Herrex' when I was talking to Dogg, yes?" Uniss asked.

"Yeah."

"Well, the Scarzen were evolved entirely for one function, that being to keep the subtle body belonging to that rogue Evercycle Herrex imprisoned. We call him H for short. Remember, I mentioned the Evercycle Council before?"

"Yeah."

"Herrex did some things awhile back and we were ordered to catch him so the Council could lock him away. His physical body is what the Scarzen unwittingly keep watch over. It takes the form of a crystal Scarzen call, Trilix, which has been part of their culture for always."

"This Herrex is really bad?" Ben asked.

"Yes, son, he's seriously the worst thing existence has come up with. It wasn't always that way though, but there is no changin' what he did now."

The line into the bunker began to move to the snorts and groans of the drommal and camel-like creatures.

"Stay close, Ben," Uniss said, plodding at the side of one drommal.

Ben looked into the long, wide entrance that reminded him of a train tunnel.

"Scarzen live nearly four times longer than you humans and are thousands of generations on from their beginnings as intelligent pack predators. Now they have developed a very sophisticated, disciplined caste culture divided into specific task groups ruled by a pyramid-style hierarchy. Everyone knows in which order they live and die and what sacrifices each must make."

"So they have families like people?"

"They call them Clan, but yes. Also, the Scarzen biology strictly has no 'he' or 'she.' Their bodies can tilt their genetics to produce or not, upon agreement, with their chosen life partner—called a Mirror."

"Called a what?"

"A Mirror, mate. One dedicated to the other for life, like ya mum and dad were. Only in the Scarzen's case, that includes the battlefield."

"Mum told Dad they had a battlefield sometimes. When they thought we couldn't hear, Mum said she thought they were like chalk and cheese a lot of the time."

"The Scarzen have a bit more of a direct approach to relations, son. They're more for actions than words."

Passing through the tunnel, Ben saw that it was lit by oil lamps every fifteen yards, which had the smell of paraffin. Thick dust quickly welled up from the ground under the pressure of hoof and foot. Then, about halfway through, dull sounds of steps on natural earth suddenly gave way to a metallic clanking. Following Uniss, Ben felt and then saw the ground surface change to metal with a rough checkerboard pattern. He noticed that the clearly defined rectangular perimeter now stretching the width and remainder of the tunnel had a single straight seam up the center. Then came his first view of the Scarzen race as they approached the sentries at tunnel's end. His eyes locked onto six heavy-set humanoid figures that had to be around eight feet tall. They inspected each of the entering travelers' wares and then waved then on through.

***

Exiting the tunnel, the wonder in Ben's mind resurfaced when the Scarzen city's interior was unveiled. Avoiding the sentries and moving beyond the shoulder of the tunnel, the oncoming street underfoot changed to a tapestry of decorative paved stonework. The view presented a round-edged cityscape in single and two-story elevations constructed of the same black stone as the perimeter walls. Every wall and surface were covered with beautiful frescoes—ornate interpretations of observed natural settings surrounding Scarzen war culture.

"Keep movin', young fella. Don't want to get stuck here."

Uniss nudged Ben to walk on to his left where he saw a choice of three streets of generous width to travel along. He felt as small as a church mouse confronted by the enormity of everything there, especially the tall and powerfully built residents. They resembled humans in general symmetry, but that's where the comparison ended. All the Scarzen had strong, chiseled features —like the stone they fashioned. With Roman noses and tattooed dark tan-reddish skin, they were all as individual as the human races of his home world.

Uniss directed Ben to take the street on the left. Ben felt his heart jump when two Scarzen walking in his direction appeared to be staring straight at him.

"Can they see us?"

He felt Uniss's hand settle on his shoulder.

"Relax, mate, like I told you, no they can't. The orange eyes are pretty off-putting at first though, aren't they? Don't worry, you'll get used to it."

When some of the Scarzen moved into the direct sunlight, Ben saw the silhouettes of powerful muscular bodies under finely made layers of clothing. He also noticed that rarely did any Scarzen footsteps make a sound, which felt eerie.

Big, deadly, and silent, Ben thought. *Maybe it's their heavy boots that mute their steps.*

"Nah, mate, it's their Scarzen skill—feather walking," Uniss told him.

Ben looked at him, having forgotten that Uniss could hear his thoughts.

"They look pretty tough, don't they?" Uniss asked. "That's 'cause they are. Those back there at the gates are standard troops, and most of the others around here now are the same. Every Scarzen in the bunker is a soldier in one way or another. As passive and domestic as they appear here going about their business, they are all highly evolved warrior strategists. As I said earlier, domestically either of a Scarzen pair can attempt birth by choice—those who have never given birth are always referred to 'he' or 'they,'. Being called 'she' is a title of privilege in Scarzen culture. When the Jenaoin pattern-makers designed Scarzen evolution, Scarzen were made very hard to kill. The only drawback in their design is, only one in seven pregnancies goes to full term. So, offspring are highly prized here—and the most precious thing in Scarzen culture, apart from trilix that is."

Ben raised an eyebrow and shook his head.

"Weird."

Uniss smiled. "You have seahorses in your world's oceans where the males have the babies, not the females, you know."

Ben looked puzzled.

"When it's time to reproduce," Uniss continued, "one Scarzen agrees to carry the offspring and tends to domestic duties in the bunker. The other continues a life in military service to the clan. Also, you should know that until the Flaxon—a rival culture here in these parts—became more evolved in metalwork and agriculture, Scarzen were on top of the food chain."

"The who?"

"Flaxon—people that look like you, son! I mentioned them earlier. That's where Dogg has gone. The Flaxon live in Flaxor, north and past the mountain range from here. You have to know, Ben, that physical models like the one you're wearing are in a lot of places. Most of them, though, are lesser evolved than your human race."

"What models? I'm not a model. I'm a person," Ben said.

"Sure you are, mate. We all often think we are something we are not. Just like every other mortal, you're wearing a . . . physical meat suit, to put it plain. So, being you is a relative term. There is a lot more to you than your fingers and toes, you'll find as we go."

"Those Scarzen look like they have armor for skin. It looks so hard, it could be rock. Some of them even have scales on their necks. Look at that one . . . and that one."

Uniss gave a short laugh. "Yeah, that they do, don't they? But don't ever tell 'em though. They won't see it as a kindness. From the neck down, armored skin does cover everything. Only their face looks like yours—well, almost. That skin they're in, that's one of the pattern-makers' finest achievements in dermal armor. Why, their skin will turn aside the point of the sharpest steel on your world."

Before Uniss could continue, an approaching Scarzen soldier caused him to steer Ben out of the way. The Scarzen wore a crimson-dyed smock with a strange symbol of an eye inside a rolling wave on the chest. The soldier passed close enough for Ben to touch. On further observation, Ben noticed that each Scarzen had a thick double spine that forked at the skull's base. The penetrating sunlight allowed a silhouetted view of many Scarzen physiques. It seemed to Ben that under the exposed skin tissue of the shoulders and neck, strong cable-like sinew crisscrossed muscle to support the skeleton. Some individuals wore silky, soft-looking tunics of many brilliant colors. Ben also thought everyone smelled like basil or curry leaves as they walked past.

As they passed an alley, Ben saw someone down the way wearing a long brown coat and a brown hat pulled so far down that Ben couldn't see the figure's eyes.

Huh. He sure doesn't look like a Scarzen, Ben thought. *Maybe another Warden like Uniss?*

The figure had his hands in his coat pockets, and the clothes he wore beneath reminded Ben of the ones the attendants wore in the Garden of Transitions. A strange pain began to pulse through Ben's chest. The figure lifted his head a bit, seemed to be aware of being watched, and darted into a nearby doorway.

Odd, Ben thought as he began to turn his head to say something to Uniss about the mysterious figure.

But then, without warning, Uniss stepped between Ben and a passing drommal on his blind side, which made Ben stagger and stumble a bit, bumping against the beast's leg joint. He felt Uniss's strong grip take hold of his arm and pull.

"Careful there, young fella! Keep your eyes ahead, okay?" Uniss pulled him out of the way of another beast following behind. "Don't want you stomped out of the game even before you have a chance to look around."

Ben caught his breath and groaned.

"There is so much to learn! My head is nearly full. Does that other Warden bloke I just saw teach as fast as you, Uniss?"

Uniss stopped and swung Ben a sharp look. Seeing nothing, he hustled Ben over against the side of a building. As other Scarzen went about their domestic business on the busy street, Uniss looked around with great suspicion, one hand on Ben's chest keeping him against the wall.

"What did he look like? Be specific," Uniss said, his tone shifting to a command.

"Well, I couldn't see his eyes with his hat pulled down. He looked a bit like the attendants in the Garden, only he walked with his hands in his pockets . . . like a gangster holding a gun. He had a long brown coat and a brown hat. And . . . it made my chest hurt just to look at him."

Ben saw Uniss's eyes grow wide.

"Where? Where did you see him?"

"In one of the alley streets we just passed. He was walking our way and stopped. He saw me watching him and turned quick into another doorway and disappeared," said Ben. "That's why I almost ran into that drommal."

Uniss sighed with a settled expression, but Ben could still feel the tension.

"You see him again, tell me straightaway," Uniss said, giving Ben a little smile. "If he ever approaches, you run—and call me as loud as you can. Got that? That's the Starlin, you heard me mention to Dogg. He is very bad news, works for someone even nastier. He'll do you great harm if he gets in arms' reach. Never trust anything he says no matter how he says it, okay, he's very dangerous, you understand?"

"Yes," said Ben.

"Right, so keep your eyes peeled and remember everything I'm tellin' you. Okay, down this side street, come on."

As they walked, Uniss put a hand to his ear. "Dogg, Starlin is here. Keep comm link to secure SAC channel Unity Delta 1. We're being tracked."

"I know," came Dogg's reply. "A House of Zero informant just told me Starlin is here looking for the Tome of Zharkaa. That can't be possible, Uniss. We saw it destroyed."

"No, Dogg. We never actually recovered the tome. We assumed the tome was destroyed when the cave-in occurred. Don't forget, when the Scarzen Brasheer cleared the space, all we found was that sinkhole and then assumed that Zharkaa and the tome were lost in it. All we managed to do was stop Zharkaa's ritual to resurrect Herrex."

"Maybe Farron can help again," said Dogg. "I'll try to contact her in the mountain without raising attention."

"With Starlin showing his face, the tome must have resurfaced—or Starlin believes he knows where it is and intends to recover it. Dogg, they're going to try to resurrect Herrex again. Find the tome before Starlin does, or we'll have more than our own atomization to worry about."

Uniss broke his transmission and touched Ben on the shoulder.

"Keep movin' mate, things just more complicated."

CHAPTER

10

Shadow Games

Uniss ushered Ben down a quieter side street.

"Like I said, Ben, you need to think on your feet. Circumstances in our job are always fluid."

"And dangerous," said Ben.

"At times, very," said Uniss. "What would an adventure be without some risk? You need to know as much as possible for things to come. We have eyes on us now not from this world, so stay vigilant."

"What does Starlin want?" asked Ben.

"Something he thinks we have that will allow him to cause a great deal of trouble. Now listen, we have a job to do. I'll explain as we go."

"Okay."

Uniss set a steady pace down the street.

"Good. So, at an average height of seven and a half to eight feet tall, these Scarzen can fill a space pretty quick when war horns sound. Their skin and bones can withstand enormous pressure and shock from blunt trauma, such as clubs and even some projectile weapons.

"Scarzen are hard to kill and don't break easily then."

"You got in one. They can run for great distances to battle as fast as a good quarter horse of your world—and fight on the run after they arrive. They even have two hearts encased in bone inside the center of their pelvis."

Ben put a hand on his stomach. "You're kidding."

"No, I'm not. They have unmatched reflexes when it comes to close combat too, along with the tenacity of a raging tiger and kill-strength of a rogue elephant when defending their space. On top of everything, Scarzen are very smart."

"Geez, have you ever had to fight them before?"

Uniss smiled and guided Ben around some covered articles against one wall.

"Not for a very long time, and you better hope we never have to either. You wouldn't amount to even an after-dinner mint for one of their standard troops. And there are lot tougher ones with pretty scary abilities other than those we see here. Other cultures here label Scarzen as demons because of a special innate ability for a thing they called, kin. Oh, here we are. Turn left."

Uniss checked to see if they were being followed.

Something doesn't feel right.

They passed by a stall selling spices and other mysteries in clay pots. To Ben's surprise, the stall next to it had bunches of orange grapes.

"Scarzen make wine from those," said Uniss.

Bunches of grapes with little blue leaves between them, hung next to many other strange fruits and vegetables that Ben had never seen.

"Scarzen foods mostly taste pretty good, young fella. Keeps 'em all fit, especially those kambaa mushrooms there. Horrible-smelling fungus the

Scarzen consider a delicacy. He pointed to a box of bluish-brown mushrooms. "Makes their breath smell like crotch rot."

"That's a vivid picture," said Ben, who avoided getting too close. "Wow! That stuff stinks." He pulled his head back sharply.

Uniss gave a chuckle and urged Ben on, walking and talking: "Scarzen have two sets of lungs that sit behind the genitals in the center of their chest."

"Their what, in their where?" Ben asked.

With a twist of a grin, Uniss pointed to Ben's crotch and then to his chest.

"In a Scarzen, those go here."

"No way."

"So, you'll have to kick a lot higher if you intended to rattle their vegetables. They're well protected behind that heavily armored chest scale. The only sure way to kill a Scarzen outright is to remove their head or penetrate their pelvic shield in one incontestable action."

"Their enemies must think messing with them is high risk," said Ben.

Uniss slowed, checked over his shoulder to see if they were being followed. He nodded.

"Everything in Scarzen culture is geared toward the day of battle, young fella, don't ever forget that."

Uniss gestured at a Scarzen purchasing some sundries at a stall nearby.

"They're good with a needle and thread too. Notice how the clothing on most citizens has the appearance of silk. It is a thread made locally from a worm called 'slaa' in Scarzen tongue. The slaa worm produces an infinitely stronger and more damage-resistant thread than human high tensile steel and it's produced naturally. They have huge groves nearby. It's one of the few things they trade with a small number of other cultures here in Ludd. They bind the fine strands together on a machine called a Torje. It's a bit like a weaving loom. The fabric is used for everything from sewing layered armor trousers and jerkin or making boots, to setting vicious snares and traps for food and enemy too."

Uniss pointed to a bolt of the fabric as they passed a corner stall.

"Here, feel this," Uniss said.

"Wow. It's soft, like wool," Ben said.

They moved on, turning right onto a wider street, then headed farther away from the market and the main gate.

"All waste is passed through one Cloaca in their behind."

"Uniss?"

"Yeah, mate?"

"Did I really need to know what they do with their Clacker?"

"It could help you someday, save your life even. Besides, I've always found Scarzen to be one of the Superverse's most fascinating biological evolutions."

"What are we looking for, anyway?"

"Clues, mate, things out of place."

"All their faces look so stern," Ben said. "They step so quiet and everyone appears so polite to one another. Are we being followed? You've looked back a couple times since we came down this street."

"Just keepin' an eye out, mate, that's all," said Uniss.

"The way they've built all this out of stone. Everything looks like one bit of rock and all the buildings have rounded corners, and there are almost no windows. It must be dark inside."

Ben arched his neck to see up the side of a building they passed.

"Not at all. Scarzen are master masons."

"How come there are no carts or carriages? How did they move big stuff about?"

"Like I said. They build everything without the use of the wheel, mate. Remember I mentioned a capability for manipulating the elements called, 'Kin,' it translates as, shock and lift. They use their kin skill like a tool, combined with an extraordinary ability in natural world engineering and fortification. Aside from the pure speed, power, and resolve in battle, they possess one other unique talent."

"What's that?"

"They are masterful negotiators and manipulators of circumstance."

"Can I smell… beer?" Ben asked. "It smells like the pub where Dad used to go."

Uniss took a sniff of the breeze passing them in the street.

"Yeah. There must be a mellow mead and wine tavern close by."

"Are the others you told me about before—the ones like people here—as strong as the Scarzen?" Ben asked.

"The Flaxon, you mean?"

"Yeah them."

"Well, they are formidable in their own right I suppose, but were evolved for different reasons. Ludd continent has many different races, Ben. Each was created for a distinct purpose. Several are humanoid in appearance. Often the similarity ends there, though." Uniss patted Ben on the shoulder. "Don't worry, you'll see. Follow that lanky-looking Scarzen carrying the roll of furs . . . to the left."

Walking along, Ben noticed the exquisitely embossed stone carvings that lined the narrow street.

"What are all the carvings on the road stones for?" Ben asked.

"Some are for decoration, others are codes in their pictorial language called 'Chicaa.' They often use them like street signs, since the city layout is so apt to change. I've been using them to be sure we are going the right way."

"That looks creepy," Ben said. He pointed to the corner of one building where a mounted sculpture in the form of a crouched potbellied gargoyle looked down upon the street. Its fierce eyes glared down from its snarling impish face.

"Oh, that. They are called, 'obi', and mark the vicinity of a keystone. It has to do with the bunker defenses. That—"

Uniss snapped his head to the right and muttered something under his breath.

"What?" asked Ben.

"Company. Come on."

He pushed Ben closer to the wall and reached behind a green climbing plant and pressed a switch. There was a clunk and then a grind of stone, and suddenly the wall behind them swung like a gate to ninety degrees, cutting off the way back. As the gate closed, Uniss watched their pursuer disappear from view. In the distance, a horn sounded and then Ben heard a rush of activity coming from several directions.

"Let's go," said Uniss. "I bought some time, but things will get very busy here soon."

Moving on, Ben noticed more of the obi statues here and there some with different strange expressions sitting on wall pillars or water runoff points near roof tops. Many of the more established merchants had a smaller Obi above their store signs that also displayed that Chicaa picture writing Uniss had mentioned. Ben thought of it as "chicken feet script." He noticed that most signs hung from cables of that bluish-black slaa thread. Now he looked for it, the stuff was everywhere.

"Have they found whoever's following us?" he asked Uniss.

"No, be unlikely. He will have dissolved from their sight by now," Uniss replied.

They walked past a short dead-end street. Noise drew Ben's attention. In a relatively small area, four armed Scarzen appeared to be in a violent combative dance and clash of arms and legs. Feeling the pressure slacken from their pursuer, Uniss let Ben take a moment to observe the opposing two on two face off.

"What are they doing? It looks awesome."

"Meld, son. They are in Meld. In Scarzen combat, each warrior can form a faultless neural link with a chosen ally close by. It allows the pair to fight as one entity. They can combine as many as five warriors using this skill. What these young ones are performing is a mock battle. You know, to hone their skills for their inevitable path as a warrior to come. It's a sort of fighting without anyone dying, and dying is something enemies of the Scarzen do a lot of when their lines are crossed."

Ben watched the four warriors exceptional grace and agility, wielding their weapons with menacing intent. Swings and thrusts at one another produced a faint whirring sound, combined with sparks when blades clashed. They wove in and around each other, working seamlessly from one posture to another. Ben's heart rate lifted watching the deadly beautiful ballet.

"It's all sort of how you might have a conversation with a close friend around here really," said Uniss.

"I only have one of those," said Ben.

"One of what?"

"Close friend. Her name is Ann. Not able to read her mind though, and I certainly wouldn't be stabbing her with any of those things."

Ben looked a little deflated, thinking he might not ever see her again, trying not to let Uniss see.

"This way," said Uniss leading him on. "Each Scarzen may only have one true battle ally that represents a life bond. They can even lend each other mental energy if the combat goes on too long and one gets fatigued or wounded. They are a hard team to beat."

"To me they seemed to be moving at a super-fast pace, thrusting, kicking, and grappling like that," said Ben. "And I've never seen anything jump like them. They'd be great basketball players, without the knives, I mean. It's a wonder no one dies right there. Can you teach me how to do that?"

"Like I said, there's a lot of stuff for you to learn mate. It's fine, those guys are clan, by their insignia on the torso armor. A blade struck against a blood family member affects their opponent only as a club would. To anyone else, however, it would be instant death or a grisly loss of limb."

"That's mad how this place is, Uniss."

Uniss pointed and guided Ben on.

"Most of the other cultures here tend to steer clear of these fellas where altercations are on the cards. Choosing to have a punch-up with a Scarzen usually means the opposition is desperate or stupid—maybe both. The cost is always high and in Scarzen favor. Battles against them tend to be short and merciless."

"You've learned a lot about them."

Uniss gave a short humph. "Had to. During the end of the Citadel Wars, Dogg and I had many dealings with the Scarzen when this planet was being made ready for its greater purpose. Some clans were adversarial back then, and much more primitive in thinking. I made one or two friends though. But, attempting to read Scarzen faces for sign of mood or intent leads most non-Scarzen into trouble. Trying to tell what they are about to do by their facial expression, is sort of like trying to tell if a grizzly bear is happy or angry by looking at its face. You can't know, until it goes to eat you or treats you with respect. The safety is, a Scarzen's word is their bond, always go by that and you'll have them well measured."

"I'll remember that," said Ben.

"There is one exception. If you ever get one sour on you and you do see a twist in their expression like a smile, it's best to run and hide. At that point, someone is about to lose body parts in a very surgical slaughterhouse kind of fashion."

Ben looked about, now feeling as though he might just be in a den of hungry lions with no way out.

Uniss touched Ben on the shoulder.

"Don't worry, mate. That's why we stay invisible. Get my drift?"

While he felt an underlying sense of fear for these Scarzen, Ben also found them fascinating.

"Notice how each Scarzen has beads or bands of gold in combinations on their braids hanging from in front and behind their ears?"

"Yeah?"

"They signify clan status, caste and military ranking. Their whole identity is in those ear braids. The custom of having their hair in one of the many dreadlock arrangements provides clues to clan identity too."

"Their culture seems very sophisticated."

"Scarzen bunkers, like the one we are in now are designed according to how Scarzen see the mind. Each bunker has its own unique layout and street labyrinth. In here, just like your thoughts, pathways can be changed at a moment's notice, just like I did back there. It was something their mystics—the Nur and Brasheer—came up with a very long time ago. And for us right now with the tail we have, we've used it to our advantage. Remember mate, brains first, always."

"Right, smarter not harder."

"Very good mate. Can I use that?"

"Sure.'

Ben noticed another one of those odd short walls Uniss activated earlier. This one jutted out toward the center of the street.

"Those moving walls are clever," said Ben.

"All the Scarzen architecture is constructed with the ability to shift or change for defensive reasons, and the smooth lines of their architecture reflect their feelings of the flow of battle. Not much farther, mate, just down here. How you doin' . . . legs warn out yet?"

"A little."

"Well, there's a sinister bloke following us intending something ugly comes our way."

"I haven't had a glass of water or breakfast. When do we get to eat? My stomach's empty."

Uniss pulled a strap of dried something out of his pocket and handed it to Ben.

"What's this?" asked Ben.

"Jeamo jerky. It will help keep your strength up."

Ben sniffed it and pulled a face.

"Smells gross."

"The live animal was a lot worse, but it'll do the trick for now."

They turned down a side alley, passing between two long buildings. Amazingly, the natural black stone somehow reflected the afternoon sunlight well. As they exited the other side of the buildings, off to their left, Ben heard a strange ringing sound. Focusing to the sound, he heard sharp cracks and bangs. A bell echoed, followed by the sound of a crowd cheering.

"Uniss, I have that weird feeling in my chest again," said Ben.

Even as he said it, Ben noticed Uniss looking to the right.

"What's wrong?" asked Ben.

Uniss took him by the arm.

"I think our friend has found his way around the obstruction." Uniss looked toward the place all the cheering was coming from. "Want to see basketball played Scarzen style?"

"Ah . . . now?"

"Come on. Maybe we can lose him in a crowd of mixed signatures."

***

Uniss and Ben crossed a wide street into a sweeping manicured garden parkland of vibrant green that stood as stark contrast to the buildings and streets of black glass stone. Seeing it took Ben completely by surprise.

"Scrape a bone, it's bigger than a soccer field," said Ben.

After moving inside a few yards, they saw that the central feature, a large amphitheater, was where all the hoopla was coming from.

"Come on," Uniss said.

They passed various abstractly-shaped hedges that reminded Ben of places he'd seen in the Garden of Transitions. Then they marched across the grounds to the edge of the amphitheater via a labyrinth of pathways where Scarzen numbers increased.

"We'll follow them, this should do the trick," said Uniss.

On the arena's rim stood lifelike stone sculptures of Scarzen warriors and other creatures alien to Ben's mind. Something caught Uniss's eye and he led the way to an obelisk where they found, carved in a sitting position, a life-sized statue of Dogg.

Ben's mouth fell open in disbelief.

"Now tell me that isn't Dogg. She's pretty popular around here, huh?" he said.

Uniss sighed, looking around.

"She said she fixed all that," he said under his breath. "Well, mate, ah . . . Dogg has a way of making herself remembered."

Ben noticed the obelisk had a Chicaa inscription covering one complete face of the stone's surface.

"What does that say?" asked Ben testing his mind link.

"It's the Scarzen first law of battle." Uniss recited, reading from the top: *"'Wars are like seasons, they inevitably come and go. It is not the volume of lives a Scarzen takes, but what a Scarzen learns from the battle that insures victory for the future.'"*

Another roar came from the crowd across the way pulling their attention. Uniss led Ben on to the center of the commotion.

***

Standing on the top stone steps Ben looked down into the entertainment structure. He thought the setting looked like a black stone whirlpool of activity with an alien game being played at the center of a main court. There seemed to be other courts beyond the one they were focused on too. It was one of the most bizarre games he could have ever imagined seeing.

"Time to hide in plain sight, mate," said Uniss. "Let's sit down over there behind that group."

Uniss directed Ben over to a large empty space a few levels down from the top rim of the amphitheater. The stadium by looks could seat several thousand Scarzen spectators comfortably, but today only half the seated area was full.

"It's a junior's game by looks," said Uniss like he'd seen many before as he sat down. "Keep your eyes peeled. Does your chest still hurt?"

Ben shook his head. "Why can't the Scarzen see who's following us, Uniss? That Starlin guy I mean."

"Because he has some of the same tricks we do, mate. He is very good at hiding in the shadows too. Have to lose him good and proper before our next destination. If he doesn't show himself in a short while we'll move on."

The crowd roared at what was happening court-side below. Occupying the entire bottom of the amphitheater, he saw an oval-shaped stone-surfaced court. He figured the center measured about half the size of an average soccer field.

He looked for the man in the brown coat, but he was nowhere to be seen and for now he welcomed the rest and distraction. A low sandstone wall traced the court's boundary a few feet outside a clear yellow line that defined the court itself.

A tall vertical net hung from posts mounted from the short wall's capstones all the way around. On the court's sideline, spaced at regular intervals around the perimeter, stood several vertical flat bronze-colored plates. Each looked just taller than the players on the court and as wide as their shoulders. Each one stood independently straight out of the stone floor with no support that Ben could see.

"What do they call this?" Ben asked.

Uniss grinned and rested his hand on Ben's shoulder, keeping an eye out for Starlin.

"This is called 'Pukecko,' mate."

On the court, Ben saw fourteen competitors: seven in red and seven in tan sleeveless loose-fitting smocks covering them from neck to mid-shin. They appeared to not be wearing armor underneath and wore the same thick black boots he had seen others wearing around the streets. The only other individuals down on the court were six figures wearing black robe-like deep-sleeved garments that made them look like mysterious high priests.

"Whatddiya think of the ref?" Uniss asked pointing to one of the individuals in black. "Not your usual whistle blowers hey."

Two stood at each end and two at opposite sides of the halfway point, all holding a purple and green flag in each hand controlling the game.

"So those guys are the refs. Right. Wondered what their job was," said Ben.

"They are simply called, the Law," said Uniss. "But they are more than that. They are skill assessors. Later they will make recommendations for postings for each player for their future in the scarzen military. Pukecko is way more than sport, mate, it is at the heart of who the Scarzen are—it's a pup's first real steps to earn respect in their martial combative culture."

"Hey . . . you're not ever expecting me to get down there with them, are you?"

Uniss tossed Ben a side glance and a wry smile then looked back to the game.

"Now listen. While we are waiting to see if Starlin shows his face, this will also double as your first lesson in Warden survival strategy and how a race not of your world thinks. As for the adolescents you're looking at now—it's the first significant step to what the Scarzen call their 'Rite of Passage to serve.'"

"Serve?"

"All Scarzen serve Scarza first, and last, Ben. Just like we Wardens serve the House of Zero first and last. See those two stone boxes with the studded mini-castle doors at either end?"

"Yeah."

"They are called 'Bunkers.' Sort of a mini reflection of the one we're sitting in now. And that yellowish line forming a triangle in front of them with the top point heading toward center court, that's called, 'the approach.' All Scarzen watch the approach carefully. Hope you're a quick study, Ben. This will be helpful later. The big fella standing inside that triangle protecting the bunker, he's the 'Warden'. Toughest and most senior competitor on the court."

"Thought you said there was no 'he' or 'she.'"

"There's not, remember I already said that 'he' can be used for any Scarzen who's not given birth."

"Now I remember," Ben said.

"So, the halfway line marked with a dot in the middle, that dot's actually a hole to eject the 'Chool,' which is what Scarzen call a ball. That's what they are hurling around right now. It's just bigger than a baseball, made from a light metal the Scarzen produce—a bit like aluminum."

"It's made of metal? That's gotta hurt."

Ben watched the players hurl the ball to each other at a breathtaking velocity. Regularly, they bounced it off the vertical metal plates around the court with a clang to another player. Each plate rang with a noticeably different tone when the chool struck it.

"That's where the bell noise we heard came from," said Ben, nodding.

"Yep, and those plates are magnetic and change polarity to hold or repel the thrown chool," said Uniss. "Each player has to recognize the change in sound and color of the rebound plate to know whether the chool will stick or bounce. Teaches them to make split second decisions and use their other senses as much as their eyes.

"I didn't think anyone could jump that high. The way they flip about and charge each other down, it's a wonder nobody gets killed."

"Life is hard on Tora, Ben. There is no place on the battlefield for weakness. This is as close as they come to sport. It's the only game they play apart from a strategy board game called 'Carrack.'"

Ben watched one player jump twice his own eight-foot height in front of an approaching opponent, attempting to recover the chool before them. Then, on descent, using a scissor kick, the airborne player struck the opponent's torso and the flying chool simultaneously. With a faint zing-fizz sound over the crowd's revelry, the ball ricocheted heavily off one of the court plates, making a dull bong and into the hand of another player. It made a sharp clap in his glove. Some of the crowd rose to their feet applauding. The infectious atmosphere had

Ben wanting to stand too, but Uniss put a hand on his shoulder to keep him in place.

"Gets to you, doesn't it?" said Uniss.

"Yep, it sure does!"

Just then, they observed a violent collision between three of the players converging in a struggle to take the chool. Although landing on the hard ground like strewn skittles after the clash, none flinched from the impact at all. Instead, they used the momentum of the collision to roll onto their feet, continuing the pursuit of the elusive chool.

"The game's title comes from a very courageous and fierce fighting bird from the southern jungles of Ludd, called a Pukecko" Uniss said, pointing near the court sideline to his right. "Look down there, there is the one for this bunker."

Ben looked at the Pukecko down below. It sat unperturbed by all the game uproar on a red cushion atop a raised dais, like royalty.

"Looks a bit like an emu, but with a much bigger head," said Ben.

Looking back to the game, Ben watched the two teams move with speed and agility that amazed him. Players hurled nearly transparent fields of force from their hands and chest to repel other players from taking advantage or to suspend the chool's progress. The crowd cheered, which made the Pukecko mascot stand and do a victory dance, wings spread.

"That's the kin skill I told you about, Ben. Only at juvenile strength. The Scarzen see the Pukecko as a resourceful and stealthy warrior, a true survivor. The bird represents both sides. It only stands when skill, tactics, and surprise to overcome the enemy and control its environment have been well executed. So your lesson here is: Only use strength as a backup; remember that, young fella."

The crowed began to chant with fists raised: "Muhindee, Muhindee, Muhindee!"

"The most famous Pukecko mascot in Scarzen history is Muhindee. It's the greatest complement a player can receive from the crowd. In Scarzen, Muhindee means, arrow of the justice."

Another roar came from the crowd, as one of the players trying to score received a mighty crushing blow by the warden guarding the bunker at the far end.

"By the time a Scarzen has graduated to become a warden, he has learned how to tactically stand his ground. A warden, like that one who just smacked the opposition in front of the bunker, is usually the oldest player. It's like a final exam in strength and resolve. The buck stops right there." Uniss emphasized that last point. "They protect the bunker blindfolded. Sometimes you too are going to have to do your duty blindfolded, and at great risk."

Uniss's comment made Ben shiver when it's meaning hit home.

"See, both wardens have a hood on. They have to rely on their teammates to do their job. Just like Dogg and I will have to depend on you now, get my drift. Sometimes we will be blind to your actions and we'll have to trust you will do the right thing when hard choices come. Can you do that, Ben?"

"I'll try my best," said Ben.

"Don't try, son, triers die in our job; succeed."

Uniss pointed to the court.

"Out there, three sets of pairs work together to cover the middle and flanks of the court just like on the battlefield. They act as the driving force at work to achieve victory. Of each pair, one is called the Shield and the other is called the Blade. Every Scarzen learns to play first as the shield, then the blade, and finally they become qualified as a warden who—"

"Protects the bunker," Ben following the thread.

"Right! You're catching on quick, good. The warden is forbidden to move outside that triangle, the approach. That teaches him to stand the line. Just like you will do the job you're given and stay within your designated task description."

"Or someone gets hurt."

"That's right. Think of yourself as one of those juveniles out there right now, Ben. After a juvenile qualifies in all three disciplines, they may play any position. That is, until they leave the care of their mother protector. In your world, that's me and Dogg now."

Ben watched two players collide and winced at the impact.

"Or mistakes like that happen," said Uniss, using the real-life visual as an example. "A warden must combine their kinetic skill set and use of the 'Solft.' That's that odd-looking staff with the ring on top that both the wardens are carrying. You are studying to be a Warden, mate, and it's going to cost you at times to get there. You're always part of a team. Teams are chosen from throughout the bunker by ballot as they come of age. This is to reflect the immediate circumstances of who is available on the day for battle and to avoid prejudice in choice." He looked at Ben and winked. "Kind of how we got you. Now, this is important. You'll notice the crowd cheers for both sides equally, which would seem strange to many other races."

"Yeah. Why do they do that?" asked Ben.

"Detachment. Something you are going to have to learn well, if you are going to succeed. To the Scarzen, the game outcome is one that represents the best interests of the bunker, not the individual, regardless of who wins here."

"So, they all defend the bunker to the last."

"Every damn last one of 'em, mate."

The crowd erupted with a resounding cheer. It made Ben almost cringe at the raw power of the noise. Watching between standing cheering spectators, he saw a red player launch themselves into a jumping cartwheel. They shoulder-crashed through the doors of the bunker right past the warden disappearing inside the stone box. His team mates rushed over to help pull him back into the light.

"Is it over?" Ben asked.

Uniss looked about.

"Yes, mate, time to go. I can't see our tail anywhere. Seems the crowd did its job and will cover our departure too. Come on, get up there in front of me and start movin'."

Uniss noted that Ben didn't appear so apprehensive now and began climbing toward the top as asked, careful not to bump into anyone.

"Did you like it?" asked Uniss.

"Sure did. Be great to see it again," Ben said, jumping up onto the grass.

"Perhaps when we're not being followed. Wait a minute, Ben."

Uniss stopped to check for Starlin again and get a bearing.

"Head on that way to your left."

"Where to now?" asked Ben.

"One of the keys to us being here, I hope," said Uniss. "Let's go, or we'll miss our appointment."

✳✳✳

They hurried on away from the pukecko court area onto another side street. It took time to cover the ground across the bunker. Chewing on a piece of the jerky Uniss gave him, Ben started to wonder if they would ever get to where they were going. He complained that the jerky tasted like shoe leather at one point, and Uniss feeling sorry for him pulled from his coat pocket what he called "special apples." The two pieces of fruit were pale green and crisp to bite.

"Only a bite here and there, mind you. It's long march food," Uniss said, "or you'll get a bellyache. Half of one for now, half for tomorrow is plenty for you to get used to, get my drift?"

Ben followed Uniss along a quiet street until they found the building he was looking for. The houses on this street were packed close together and often two stories high. The house in front of them looked to be still under construction on one side. Uniss checked around for Starlin and gestured to the olive-green stone house.

"Right, no sign of him and here we are," Uniss said with expectation in his tone. "Stay close."

Uniss stepped forward through an elegantly-crafted wrought-iron gateway with Ben in tow. They walked through the building's open front entrance and out the back. About thirty long steps across the way, several Scarzen stonemasons worked on a part of a stairway to another inner keep. The stairs sat in the center of a labyrinth of low hedging and Uniss remarked that it was a central feature of the space. The surrounding gardens were well manicured and used hedges to isolate different sections of the area. A soft lawn covered everywhere else instead of the common black stone used in so many other places Ben had seen. Stone seats were sparsely placed at opposite ends of the courtyard.

"There's the one we are interested in, Ben. The one on the left," Uniss said, pointing to a pair of Scarzen masons working on the stone stairway. "His birth name is Beetaa Pinnaraa."

Ben looked with interest.

"This Scarzen has the potential to change the entire course of history on this world in the near future and ultimately the Superverse beyond."

"Wow. Why is he so important?"

"We are here to observe all the things connected to this young warrior. It will also help us understand what Starlin is doing here following us. As you can see, Beetaa is about the age of those you saw on the pukecko court. I'd say about forty cycles of their sun old."

The Scarzen that Uniss indicated stood less than average height for an adolescent and displayed a lanky physique.

"He's not as tall and muscular as most of the others," Ben said. "But he looks just as strong the way he swings that hammer."

"You're right about that, but that Scarzen—he has more potential in kin skill than a dozen of the best in his clan combined. And you know what else?"

"What?"

"Beetaa is completely unaware of it at this time. Right now, he looks forward to an ordinary Scarzen's life among the ranks of his peers doing their bit, kinda like you were. I'm inclined to believe this one would opt to be a mother protector when permission to breed is given. Unfortunately for them, the karmic thread they belong to has them changing the course of Scarzen culture instead."

"Wow! That sounds big," said Ben.

"Yeah, depending on the decisions they will make, soon Beetaa's impact will be enormous and will stretch beyond his days. To put that in perspective, the average Scarzen lives a lifespan of some 220 standard Earth years."

"Crikey, that's a long time to be standin' on the same two legs," said Ben.

"Not really, comparatively, the Tronk of Yanick 5 can live up to 16,000 of your years before they cast their physical body aside for another cycle. So, by the time you are a granddaddy, a Scarzen like this young pup will just be moving into their prime. Beetaa is from Pinnaraa Clan, and there'll be history to be made between you two if my gut feeling is correct. So stay sharp, wouldn't want you two getting off on the wrong foot."

What does that mean? "This gets weirder by the minute," said Ben.

"Beetaa's teacher father or who they call an 'Otaa' was one of the most famous Scarzen Sentinel warriors in their recorded histories. Benataa, as he was known, was a Brasheer. You'd probably think of them as a form of sorcerer-knight."

"He was a Brasheer?" asked Ben.

"Yeah, he died in a blaze of glory some time back, when Beetaa was very young. Left his mark good and proper though."

"Beetaa lost his dad too then," said Ben.

"Yes mate," said Uniss. "Pinnaraa Clan has high standing in Scarzen culture everywhere, not just here. Their ancestors have honored the battlefield many times and distinguished themselves over and over. When a Scarzen can no longer attend the ranks for the battlefield, they go into a stage of life known as 'wise service to the bunker.' There, they pass on the skills and knowledge they have acquired to the up-and-coming, teaching according to their caste. We have to stick close to Beetaa until an appropriate opportunity presents itself."

"What opportunity?" Ben asked, looking over his shoulder at Uniss.

"Seeing something that can shed light on how those who oppose us intend to liberate the prisoner Herrex, whose body is incarcerated on this planet."

"That's sounds ominous."

"More than you know. Beetaa is the key to finding that out. Look! They're finishing work. Keep up, let's follow them," Uniss said, moving toward Beetaa. "Things are about to get interesting, mate. Our mission just went hot."

About the Author

Yuan Jur served in the Australian military as a young adult. He later sought the solitude of monastic life serving the community as an ordained Buddhist monk for many years. In Buddhism's warrior-caste arm known in the West as Zen he achieved the rank of abbot and theologian. As a theologian, Yuan Jur studied many belief systems, doctrines and ideologies from around the world. During those decades he also gained a master's degree in Chinese martial arts and medieval weaponry.

In 2007 a life threatening illness ended his monastic career and nearly his life. During recovery, Yuan Jur turned to a new venture. He combined his knowledge gained from decades of belief systems study with a love of Time Travel Paranormal alt/world fantasy as a young man. The result was a totally new immersive superverse series called Citadel 7. By 2014 his first Citadel 7 series combined trilogy had won both blue ribbon and Grand Prize in the Chanticleer Cygnus international writing Awards. He states: "There is a lot, lot more to come."

Postscript

What is Starlin's true purpose on Tora? What does he want with Uniss and Ben?

What is Uniss's real plan for Ben's future and what will the liberation of the mysterious prisoner Herrex mean?

Find out more as the story of the Citadel 7 Superverse unfolds in Novella 2, Betrayer.

Join Yuan Jur and the Citadel 7 crew at: www.citadel7online.com